The Wrong Girl

THE 1ST FREAK HOUSE TRILOGY
#1

C.J. ARCHER

CHAPTER 1

Windamere Manor, Hertfordshire, November 1888

To say I'd been kept prisoner my entire life in an attic wasn't quite true. It was only fifteen years out of eighteen, and I was allowed to walk in the gardens for a half-hour some days. Besides, the attic rooms of Windamere Manor covered the top-most floor of the entire west wing, and Violet and I had the run of them.

Nor did we want for anything. As little girls, we had every doll and toy we could desire. As young women, we had music and books, embroidery and sewing, and an education from the finest tutors. Lord Wade was generous in all things, except, of course, his love and attention toward Vi, his daughter.

She tried to pretend that it didn't matter, but I knew better. She couldn't hide her melancholy from me, or her desire to be rid of the affliction that stopped her from taking her place as the eldest of Lord Wade's children in the outside world. I saw it in her watery eyes as she gazed out the window and the way she hugged herself upon seeing the fresh burns in the Oriental rug. The latter only came after one of her episodes. The trinkets and tutors couldn't replace her parents, and in many ways she and I were both orphans, although I, Hannah Smith, was the only true one.

As prisons go, the attic of Windamere was pleasant enough, and as the orphaned daughter of servants with a strange affliction of her own to endure, I was more fortunate than most in my situation. I'd read the stories by Mr. Dickens. I knew a child of my class could wind up in the cruel workhouses if they were lucky, and the friendless streets if they were not. I'd been given a roof over my head, food in my belly, an education to rival any lord's daughter and a dear friend in Vi. Indeed, she was more like a sister than friend. She cared for me when I awoke from my unpredictable slumbers, disoriented and sluggish with a gaping hole in my memory. She was always nearby and had been for as long as I could recall.

What more could I—dare I—want?

I had just woken from one of those deep, dense sleeps when Miss Levine, our governess, stalked into our attic parlor, her black woolen gown so heavy that the skirt didn't even ripple as she moved. Her lashless eyes narrowed as she took in Vi and me sitting on the floor, holding each other. Her nostrils, two small caves at the end of a beakish nose, flared wider as she sniffed the acrid, smoky air. At such moments she resembled a rat with her sharp face and equally sharp eyes. Vi and I used to giggle behind our hands when we were little and make jokes about her rattiness. It was an attempt to stave off our fear, both of Miss Levine and of what caused the scorch marks. But we hadn't made any jokes in a long time, not since Miss Levine overheard us once and struck me with a cane until I apologized. I'd been ten years old at the time.

"At least you spared the wall hangings," Miss Levine said, her tone brisk. "A small mercy for which Lady Wade will no doubt be thankful. She doesn't have time to be furnishing these rooms, you know. She has the rest of the house to consider."

I felt Vi tense. Lady Wade, her mother, never visited us in the attic—something for which we were both grateful. It was enough to have to put up with ratty Miss Levine's moods. At least our governess had enough passion in her to grow angry on occasion. Lady Wade was simply indifferent to our plight, and that indifference made her as bleak as a February night.

"I'm sorry, Miss Levine," Vi whispered, lowering her head so that her forehead touched mine. She tucked a strand of my curly red-gold hair behind my ear, but it sprang free again. "I couldn't stop it."

Her grip tightened around my shoulders, and I pulled her closer. It was difficult to tell who was comforting whom. Perhaps it was a little of both. As always, I soothed Vi after she almost set the attic on fire, and she soothed me as I fought my way out of the fog of my narcolepsy. Our twin afflictions, seemingly intertwined with one another's, were inexplicable as much as they were dangerous.

"Stop apologizing to her," I whispered. "You can't help what happened and she knows it." It was an old refrain, spoken over and over, but it was one I felt compelled to repeat. Perhaps one day Vi would listen and cease apologizing for something she couldn't control.

"Get up, Miss Smith," snapped Miss Levine. "You are not an invalid." She waved a hand at the black scorch mark near the edge of the rug. "Attend to that."

"I'll do it," Vi said, rising. She held out her hand and I took it, although I already felt stronger and didn't need her assistance.

When I first woke from my strange slumbers, as I called my episodes, I felt vague, like I wasn't altogether *there*. It was as if I were drifting through a dream, and my head might as well have been stuffed full of cotton. After a few minutes, my head slowly cleared, and I could function normally again. Usually by then Vi had inadvertently set something alight. She claimed her episodes were brought on by her fear for me in my comatose state, but I'd never been quite convinced that was the case. It didn't make sense, although Vi certainly was afraid for me. That I didn't doubt. Poor, dear Vi was always afraid. It was why she needed me.

"No, I will." I squeezed her hand. "Go and rest on the settee, Lady Violet."

Her mouth twisted at my teasing. She didn't like me calling her by her full title. "You're too good to me, Hannah."

"She's lazy is what she is." Miss Levine wrapped her bony fingers around my arm so tightly I could feel my blood bank up in my veins. "Water, Miss Smith. Now."

I jerked free and set my feet apart to give myself a steadier stance. I might be slight in stature and Miss Levine tall, but I would not make it easy for her to push me about. I turned eighteen last month, and Vi a few months before that. We were no longer children. If anything, Miss Levine should be concerned that she'd lose her position now that neither of her charges needed her. I, on the other hand, was indispensable to Vi's happiness. For as long as she was confined to the attic, I would be with her.

"The fire's already out," I said. "There's no need for water."

"Nevertheless, I've asked you to fetch it," Miss Levine said.

"Actually, you didn't ask, you ordered."

"Do not test me, Miss Smith." Then Miss Levine did something I hadn't expected. She heaved a deep sigh. It caused her usually rod-straight back to curve, her shoulders to stoop. "We don't have time for your stubbornness. It's time for your walk. You don't want to miss that, do you? I know how you like to go out. Especially of late." Her lips curled back in what I suspected was an attempt at a smile, although I'd never actually seen her smile before, and I couldn't think what she found amusing about our walk on this particular day. "Fetch some water and make sure the fire is completely out. You know what'll happen if the floor beneath the rug is smoldering."

I knew. Three years ago, after a particularly bad attack, Vi had set the wood-paneled wall behind one of the woolen hangings alight and the flames had quickly spread.

Fortunately the fire was extinguished before it did too much damage, but only because several pails were kept full of water at all times. Afterward, Lord Wade had ventured up to the attic to inspect the damage. The next day, we'd received new hangings. It was the last time Lord Wade had visited us.

Out of the corner of my eye, I saw Vi sink onto the settee as if her knees had given way. She turned her pale face to stare out the parlor's only window. While we both loved looking at the scenery through that window and making up stories about the people we saw coming and going from the house, she hated venturing outside for our walks. She seemed especially anxious today. Indeed, her nervousness had grown worse after I'd spotted the handsome gardener watching us. I, on the other hand, had been curious. Poor Vi. She was as much imprisoned by her fears as by her father.

I did as I was told and dipped the jug into one of the pails of water lined up between the small fireplace and the door.

I splashed the water from the jug over the burned patch, getting some of it on the hem of my gray woolen skirt. I checked under the rug—also woolen—but the floorboards had been spared.

Wool. It was everywhere. Sometimes I felt like I was drowning in the stuff. Woolen rugs on the floor, woolen hangings on the walls, woolen coverings on the chairs, settees and beds. My clothes were made of wool, even in summer, as were Vi's and Miss Levine's. Everything flammable was kept in chests and drawers, all draped in woolen fabric of course. I was convinced that we were single handedly responsible for the English wool market's profits. It doesn't burn you see. Not properly. It smolders when a flame is put to it, but once the flame is extinguished, there is nothing left but a blackened scar.

The attic, and we two girls, had been smothered in wool. Just once I wanted to wear a flimsy organdy gown like the ones worn by Lady Wade and her other daughter. I'd seen them through the window from the room we used as a parlor. The window looked down on the front steps of Windamere, and the long, straight avenue lined by ancient oaks that eventually swallowed the drive in the distance.

Sometimes I looked through the window at the gentle curve of hills and the thick woods at the edge of the vast Windamere estate and wished I was out there, exploring the world, meeting people, tasting freedom.

But I couldn't leave Vi behind to live in the attic with only Miss Levine for company. Nor could Vi come with me, not with her condition. While my narcolepsy was a danger only to me, her fire starting was a danger to others. She needed my company.

Besides, where else could I go?

"Put on your coats, girls," said Miss Levine, standing at the door. "It's cool outside."

"I'll be all right," I said, taking Vi's hand. She shook her head very slightly in warning. I grinned at her. Vexing Miss Levine was a favorite pastime of mine since she no longer used her cane to punish us.

Vi chewed her lower lip and the action reminded me of something, but I couldn't quite recall what. Something at the edge of my memory, something to do with vexing Miss Levine and the worried look on Vi's face.

But the memory slipped away before I could grasp it, and I didn't bother trying to reclaim it. My memories rarely returned after my narcoleptic episodes, and I'd come to accept that they never would.

"I know you enjoy being tiresome, Miss Smith," our governess said with an exasperated sigh, "but perhaps just this once you can put on your coat without argument. Gloves and hats too."

I opened my mouth to tell her I wouldn't wear gloves, but Vi frowned. "Please do as she says without quarreling."

My hands dropped to my sides and I blinked at her. She rarely spoke to me with such vehemence, or to Miss Levine for that matter. Vi was the sweet-natured one, the peacemaker. She never challenged Miss Levine's commands, never gainsaid an order. While it was the thing I loved about her the most, it irritated me in equal measure. She was Lady Violet Jamieson, daughter of the Earl of Wade. She shouldn't be taking orders from anyone, let alone a governess.

"Vi? What's wrong?"

Her blue eyes softened and she bit her lip. "I'm sorry. I didn't mean to snap."

"You didn't." I tucked a strand of her dark red hair behind her ear as she had done with mine earlier. Where my unruly locks had refused to stay, hers remained. How I admired her sleek hair, her creamy skin and beautiful face. She would have been the belle of the ball if she'd been allowed to attend one. She was the opposite of me in so many ways. I was short and small, my face freckled. Although we both had red hair, mine was pale and orange— orange!—whereas hers was a rich mahogany.

Miss Levine clapped her hands. "Quickly now, before the weather changes. The sky is already looking quite gray in the west."

"Perhaps we shouldn't go out," said Vi.

Miss Levine gripped Vi's arm and gave her such a withering glare that my friend's face crumpled. "It's too late to change our minds now."

For once, I was in accord with Miss Levine. "If the weather changes and sets in, we may not get out again for days." I crossed the landing to our shared bedroom and retrieved our coats, hats and gloves from the brass hooks near the door. The maids had already been through. The beds were made and the hearth free of ash. The servants at Windamere were an efficient, silent lot. I hardly ever saw them let alone heard them going about their business, yet everything was spotless.

I handed Vi her things and put on my coat and hat, but not my gloves. Those I carried. I was halfway down the stairs before Vi even set foot on the top step. She was stalling, but I wouldn't let her fears keep me indoors. Not when it may be the last walk for some time with winter just around the corner, and not with the possibility of seeing that handsome gardener again, the one who watched me with such intensity that my skin prickled and my heart did little somersaults in my chest.

I waited for Vi and Miss Levine on the second-floor landing. They eventually caught up, and the governess gave me one of her stern looks. She was breathing much too hard to verbally reprimand me.

"Please slow down, Hannah," Vi said, drawing alongside me. "They'll be watching."

'They' were the invisible yet ever-present servants. Vi always worried they would gossip about us, or be staring at us, the two peculiar girls who lived in the attic.

"Let them," I said. I took her hand, and together we walked down the grand staircase to the entrance hall. The *tap tap* of our shoes on the tiles echoed around the marble hall and bounced off the columns that reached to the high ceiling, two levels above us. I glanced to my left, through the double doors into the opulent dining room beyond. It was a habit of mine when I came downstairs. The grand hall and adjoining dining room were the only two areas of the house I'd seen other than the attic, and for all I knew, the rest of Windamere Manor was nothing like those rooms. I couldn't help comparing what I saw to our attic. Our sparse, wool-covered, low-ceilinged space couldn't be further removed from the dining room. Slender statues of Roman goddesses were tucked into carved niches, and touches of gilding here and there broke up the pristine white of the walls and mantel. There was a rug too, but it was free of burns and nothing covered the large mahogany table or sideboard.

"Good afternoon, Lady Violet," said the stiff butler, Pearson. He opened the front door and bowed, revealing his bald patch. "Enjoy your walk."

"Th-thank you," Vi stuttered. Her face flushed to the roots of her hair, and her grip tightened on my hand.

"Good afternoon, Pearson," I said breezily. He hadn't addressed me, but sometimes, when I was feeling particularly irreverent, I cast aside the rules of propriety. I was, after all, a prisoner, a narcoleptic and a companion to a lady who started fires with her mind. Propriety was the least of my concerns.

It must have been the prospect of seeing *him* again that fueled my impish mood. The tall, dark-haired gardener with the intense gaze and handsome face had occupied my thoughts ever since I'd first noticed him on our walk almost two weeks earlier. I'd seen him every time we'd taken a turn in the garden since. When I'd asked Miss Levine his name she'd dismissed my question with a flick of her skeletal fingers.

"Where shall we go?" I asked Vi. "Down to the lake or across the park?" It wouldn't matter which way we went. He would be there. I knew it as surely as I knew my name was Hannah Smith.

Without waiting for an answer, I steered Vi down the terraced garden, Miss Levine trailing behind. That was another reason I enjoyed our walks. Although Miss Levine was always in attendance, she stayed a few paces back, giving Vi and I privacy.

"The sky looks rather ominous," Vi said, stopping abruptly. She cast a glance over her shoulder and I followed her gaze, just in time to see a pale face disappear from a window on the first floor. I didn't know which room the window looked into, but I did recognize the face. It belonged to Vi's fifteen year-old sister, Eudora.

Vi and I had never met her, having been condemned to the attic together when Eudora was born, and not meeting her even once on our walks. When we'd first seen her watching us through the window some ten years ago, Miss Levine had informed us that she was Vi's sister. It was the first we'd heard about her. We'd not even heard her crying as a baby.

I suspected Eudora had been ordered to stay away from us. The only other times I'd seen her was when I looked out the window as she'd left to walk or ride around the estate or to step into one of her father's carriages.

"Nonsense," I said cheerfully. "It's lovely out. Those clouds are miles away." It was an optimistic statement. The entire sky just beyond the house was as black as night, the low clouds heavy with rain. The sun, however, still shone on Windamere's façade, bathing it in a golden glow it didn't deserve.

The mansion was a statement of architectural perfection from the previous century when an ancestor of the current earl had built it. Wide and rectangular, it was all straight lines and right angles. The dozens of windows were precisely the same distance apart on all its three levels, and the grand front porch was placed exactly in the middle, the columns holding up the portico like soldiers keeping guard. Nothing was irregular or wrong at Windamere.

Nothing, that is, except Vi and I.

"Continue, girls," barked Miss Levine. "Violet! Don't stop now."

Violet held the brim of her hat and led the way across the park toward the woods. The breeze ruffled the feathers attached to the hatband, and a strand of my hair fluttered against my cheek.

"You're looking for him, aren't you?" Vi said as I drew alongside her.

"Don't be ridiculous."

"You shouldn't. You know nothing about him."

"What has that got to do with anything?"

She held the lapels of her coat together at her throat for warmth. "He could be dangerous. He could be waiting behind the bushes to..."

I snorted. "Vi, stop worrying. What do you think he's going to do with you and Miss Levine here? Ravish me?" I laughed at the absurdity of it, but even so, my scalp tingled at the thought of the new gardener kissing me.

"It's not a joke, Hannah." We'd almost reached the edge of the woods, and she stopped again, eyeing the bank of trees as if they would stretch out their branches and capture us. "It'll start raining soon."

"You want to turn back, don't you?"

She looked down at her boots and said nothing.

"Come on," I said. "The exercise will do you good. Cool that fire within you." I smiled at my little joke, but she only frowned harder. I winced. "Sorry."

"If you're determined to have your walk, then let's walk." Her tone was curt, crisp, so like Miss Levine's. "I want to go into the woods today."

"Really? I thought you hated the woods."

I glanced back at Miss Levine. She still followed, her gaze focused not on us but on the trees.

I tilted my face into the cool breeze and a fat raindrop exploded on my cheek. "Bloody hell."

"Hannah!" Vi scolded. She hated my occasional outburst, but she was used to them nevertheless and no longer truly shocked.

"We'd better hurry," I said, walking faster, clutching my gloves tighter. Another raindrop splashed on the end of my nose, then another and another. "We need to find shelter. Shall we head towards the orangery instead?"

"No!"

I blinked at her. Her vehemence was so odd, so unlike her.

"The woods are closer." She set off at a run toward the trees, and I followed. She was correct in that the thick canopy would provide some shelter against the rain. I didn't look around to see if Miss Levine followed until I reached the trees, and when I did, I was surprised to find that she was not with us.

"We should wait here for her," Vi said, breathing hard as she caught up to me.

I squinted through the rain and shook my head. "I can't see her. She must have decided to run to the orangery." The image of Miss Levine running anywhere was rather absurd, but it was odd that I couldn't see her. Wherever she'd gone, it wasn't toward us.

"The woodsman's cottage isn't far from here." Vi had to shout to be heard above the rain splattering against the leaves. "Let's wait for her there."

"I don't particularly care to wait for Miss Levine anywhere," I said. "But let's go anyway. We'll enjoy our temporary freedom, and get out of this weather." I set off along the path that had been hacked through the ferns and other bushes.

Vi's footsteps thudded on the damp leaves and earth behind me. Although we moved as quickly as we could, we were both drenched by the time we reached the old woodsman's cottage in the clearing. I pushed open the door and stumbled inside, Vi at my heels. She slammed the door, shutting out the wind and rain, but not the cool dampness.

Calling the building a cottage was perhaps a stretch. It was more like a hut, with only one room and one fireplace with a dented pot nestled among the ashes. The cottage must have stood in that clearing for centuries. The blackened beams hung low overhead, and the daub had come away in patches, revealing a skeleton of thin branches that held the walls up by some miracle. A small chest to one side of the fire contained tin bowls, cups, cutlery and a pan, and placed strategically in front of the hearth were two chairs.

"Good lord, I'm soaked!" I removed my coat and threw it and my gloves over the back of a chair.

Vi glanced around. "We're alone."

"You sound surprised."

"I...I thought the gardeners may have sheltered here too."

The gardeners did indeed use the cottage to store equipment or their packed lunch if they worked nearby, and we usually knocked before going inside, just in case. But, despite the rain and the need for shelter, the single-room cottage was unoccupied.

"I wouldn't be surprised if someone comes," Vi said.

One could only hope. I wouldn't mind seeing that new gardener again, although I was sure he wouldn't remain once he discovered us there. A male servant confined in a small space with Lady Violet would tarnish her reputation and be cause for malicious gossip if discovered.

The fact that I worried about her reputation was laughable considering she was unlikely ever to enter Society and had no need of a reputation, either good or bad.

"They must be working farther away today," I said.

Vi glanced out the window and hugged herself as a shudder wracked her. "The rain seems to have set in. We should start a small fire if we're to be here awhile." She inspected the wood box near the hearth. "There's no kindling. Will you fetch some, Hannah?"

Pity she couldn't set alight the thick piece of timber she removed from the box with a point of her finger. At least that would be a benefit to an affliction that made her life miserable.

I ventured out again. The wind slammed the door closed behind me and lashed my damp skirt to my legs. It tugged my hair out from beneath my hat and drove the cold needles of rain into my cheeks. The tired, drooping porch did little to protect either me or the neat stack of wood near the door. Hopefully the kindling inside the box fared better.

I bent to open the lid, but stopped when I saw something move out of the corner my eye. I turned to look. Nothing there except trees and rain. I straightened.

Someone grabbed me from behind. A hand holding a cloth clamped over my nose and mouth. A sweet smell swamped me and clung to the back of my throat. I tried to scream, but what little sound came out would not have reached Vi. I scrabbled at the hand, tried to pull it away, but my attacker was too strong. His other arm circled my waist, holding me against his body. I knew it was a man. No woman was built like a steel brace.

The sweet smell filled my head, my lungs, and I began to feel myself drifting into a fog. A sudden wave of panic lent me strength. I clawed at that bare hand again. The man's breath hissed through his teeth as I peeled off some of his skin with my fingernails, but my fight was all too brief. The fog closed around me. My eyelids were too leaden to keep open.

"It's all right, Lady Violet," he said. His words vibrated through the back of my head, pressed into his chest. "You'll come to no harm if you cooperate."

I felt myself slipping away. I could no longer stand and he picked me up. I would have been able to see his face if I could only open my eyes. Yet I was not so concerned about his identity at that moment as I was about what he'd just called me.

He thought I was Vi. He might be carrying me away from her, but I could still protect her. I would not tell him he had the wrong girl.

CHAPTER 2

I didn't have to open my eyes to know I was in a carriage traveling at a fast clip along a rough road. The cabin rocked and bumped violently, tossing me about on the seat upon which I half lay. My feet were on the floor, but my body was covered by a blanket. Both the blanket and my clothes smelled of damp wool, possibly the worst smell in the entire world. No, not entirely true. Whatever had been soaked into that rag and caused me to blackout at the cottage was now the worst smell ever. Still, damp wool was unpleasant and, along with the rocking cabin, made my stomach churn.

"Here, use this," a voice said.

I cracked open my eyes to see a young woman of about my own age sitting across from me. It was dim in the cabin, but I could see she was quite pretty in a quiet way that didn't strike you immediately. She had a wide mouth and bright eyes that sparkled even in the dimness. I guessed them to be blue to go with her hair color, but it was impossible to tell if they were dark like mine or paler.

She was beautifully dressed too in a pale pink gown trimmed with black lace and a tall black hat perched loftily on her blonde head. She emptied the contents of her reticle in her lap and passed it across the gap between us.

"I'm fine," I rasped, my throat dry.

The carriage lurched again and my stomach dipped and rose. I took the reticule just in time to throw up in it. Good lord, were all carriage rides so turbulent?

When I finished, I closed the reticule and hesitantly held it out for her. She screwed up her nose and shrank into her seat.

"Please don't take offense," she said, "but I don't suppose you'd mind holding it until we reach our destination. It won't be long now."

I slowly sat up and lifted the green velvet curtain edged with gold lace. The landscape whipped past at a rate that had my stomach rolling again. I'd not thought anything could move so swiftly! I let the curtain fall back into place, but not before I'd seen that it was still raining, albeit with less ferocity.

"Do you feel better?" the woman asked.

"Not particularly."

Her face fell. "Oh. It's just as well you still have my reticule then."

"Most fortuitous."

She must have heard the sarcasm in my voice because a small crease appeared between her eyebrows. "I know this is very trying for you, Lady Violet, but I want to assure you that you have nothing to fear. We don't intend to harm you."

Did I just imagine the slight emphasis on the word 'intend,' and the shifting of her gaze so that she wasn't quite looking me in the eyes? "Then you won't mind answering my questions," I said, sounding bolder than I felt.

"I don't mind, but unfortunately I'm forbidden to do so."

"Forbidden? By whom?"

She gave me a tight smile. "All will be explained when we arrive, Lady Violet."

Hearing Vi's name only deepened my sense of dread. What would they do when they discovered I wasn't Vi? What did they want her for in the first place? Ransom money? Yes, that must be it.

"Don't worry," she said as I shrank into the corner. "It's nothing sinister, and our reasons are noble. Indeed, we wish to help you." She squeezed her lips as if trying to hold back more words. I got the feeling she wasn't supposed to have said that much.

I swallowed. The lingering taste of bile burned my throat. Bile and fear. My heart hammered in my chest and I desperately wanted to go back, to see Vi again and Windamere. I'd even settle for seeing Miss Levine and my small bed. Just something, or someone, familiar. I wished I could take back every moment in which I'd craved to be far away from the attic. I suddenly felt terribly ungrateful for everything I'd been given.

I wondered how long it had taken Vi to notice I was gone. What had she done when she realized I wasn't coming back? Had she run to the house and alerted her father? Would he have listened to her and sent out a search party or ordered her to return upstairs to the attic?

It was possible that Lord Wade cared nothing about my disappearance. I was, after all, nothing more than his daughter's friend. The only person in the world who cared whether I lived or died was Vi, a prisoner in her own home and quite powerless to search for me. One thing I did know for certain—she would be utterly miserable without me, just as I felt utterly miserable and alone without her, despite the presence of the mystery woman across from me.

"I'm Miss Sylvia Langley," she said, as if she could read my mind. "Pleased to make your acquaintance."

Politeness dictated that I give my name in response, even if it were already known, but I was in no mood to be polite, nor did I want to lie and introduce myself as Lady Violet Jamieson, daughter of Lord Wade. But I certainly did *not* want to give her my real name and divulge that she had the wrong person. Whereas I could endure a kidnapping, and more, Vi's nerves would snap altogether and ruin her fragile mind.

"You seem quite certain I won't attack you and try to

escape," I said instead.

"Why would you want to escape?" She seemed genuinely puzzled. "You'll be offered a great deal more freedom than you were given at Windamere Manor."

"'A great deal more freedom' doesn't have quite the same meaning as 'You're free to come and go as you please.'"

Miss Langley's jaw went rigid. "I know your father has kept you in the attic. I would consider anything other than a genuine prison cell 'more freedom,' wouldn't you?"

So she knew that much. Interesting. It was no secret that Lord Wade's eldest daughter lived in the attic of Windamere with her governess and companion, but most thought she was there of her own volition. Even our tutors had been under the impression. Miss Levine had told us it was generally thought Vi was simple-minded and wanted to be left alone. Her stuttered greetings to the butler certainly did nothing to dispel the rumors. What everyone thought of me being kept in the attic with her, I couldn't guess. Perhaps, being the orphan of servants, they thought my situation was a fortunate one. Sometimes I believed that too.

"I'm sorry if you think Lord Wade will pay your ransom," I said. "You're going to be quite shocked when you discover he doesn't care enough to capitulate to your demands."

She lifted one brow. "You don't think he would pay a ransom for your release?"

"Do you think a gentleman who keeps his child in the attic would want her back?" Whether he did or didn't, wasn't the point. The point was, Miss Langley and her friends had not kidnapped his daughter. They'd kidnapped Hannah Smith. A nobody. Vi might not consider me replaceable, but I wouldn't begin to know what Lord Wade thought.

"I see what you mean," she said. "Well then. It's fortunate that we don't want his money, or we'd be in a pickle."

No ransom? How curious. "Then what do you want with me?"

"I am sorry, but I cannot answer any more questions." The carriage slowed and she pulled the curtain back. "Ah, here we are. Home at last."

I lifted my side of the curtain just as the carriage passed through an iron gate. Tall, thick oaks lined the drive, their overhanging branches shielding what little light filtered through the gray clouds. I caught a glimpse of a lake where bare weeping willow branches cried into the still, flat surface. Beyond that, what looked to be a ruined building rose out of the ground liked jagged teeth. It was too far away for me to see what sort of structure it had once been, or if indeed it was a genuine ruin or a folly like the one in Windamere's park.

We rounded a gentle bend and the trees thinned out until all that was left was a neat lawn and some low shrubs clipped into the shape of inverted drips. Gravel crunched under tires, and the driver urged the horses to slow with a few commanding words.

Was he the one who'd captured me? Or had my kidnapper remained at Windamere after delivering me to the carriage?

I ceased wondering as the house rolled past the window. No, not house, mansion. Or more particularly, a castle. Where Windamere Manor was all formal regularity, this house was not. There were gabled roofs in abundance, their peaks topped with decorative pinnacles like insect antennae. The gables were broken up by castellated turrets and towers, and I couldn't even begin to count the chimney stacks, there were so many. The dark gray stone was also in contrast to Windamere's golden hues, and with the heavy clouds hanging low overhead, it looked rather medieval and altogether forbidding.

A shiver trickled down my spine. "What is this place?"

"Freak House," Miss Langley said.

"Pardon?"

The carriage door opened and, because I was leaning on it, I tumbled out without an ounce of grace. I managed to hang onto the reticule as strong hands caught me by the upper arms, saving me from a muddy puddle. It had stopped raining, but the ground was drenched.

"Thank you." I looked up, straight into the green eyes of the new Windamere gardener. "You!"

He let go, but not before I noticed how warm his hands were, even through my sleeves. "My apologies," he said. "I feel terrible about what happened, but it was necessary. Or so I was I told." This last he muttered under his breath, but it didn't disguise his voice, so deep and rumbling. I remembered how it had vibrated through me when he'd grabbed me outside the woodsman's cottage. It must have been he who'd captured me and held that God-awful cloth to my nose. "Are you all right?" he asked. "No lasting effects from the ether?"

"None at all." I held out the reticule full of vomit. "Would you mind carrying my luggage?"

A small frown creased his brow as he took the reticule and glanced at Miss Langley behind me.

She giggled. "I do believe I like you already, Lady Violet." She hooked her arm through mine and I found it comforting, despite my apprehension.

Comfort or no, I released myself and took a step away from her and the gardener. They were my captors. No matter how polite or kind, I must always remember that they'd kidnapped me using unconscionable methods.

Miss Langley chewed her lower lip and looked as if she'd burst into tears. "*Say* something to her, Jack."

The gardener stared at me, and for a brief moment, I saw a sadness in his eyes that equaled Vi's on days when I couldn't drag her away from the window. But it was so fleeting that I wondered if I'd imagined it. "I suspect anything I say will sound hollow." Although he answered Miss Langley, I felt as if he spoke directly to me.

"You could introduce yourself," I said. "That would be a good place to start."

It must not have been the response he expected because he took a moment to answer and his mood seemed to lighten a little. "Jack Langley at your service." He bowed.

"Langley? You are brother and sister?"

"Cousins," Miss Langley said.

"I see. And will *you* tell me why I've been brought here against my will, Mr. Langley?"

"All will be revealed soon enough," he said.

I glanced from him to his cousin. She smiled unconvincingly. "As I already told Miss Langley, Lord Wade will not pay a ransom for my return. He simply doesn't care enough. Why would he when he has a perfect daughter in Eudora?" I bit the inside of my cheek to stop myself blabbering. The Langleys didn't know about the fire starting. How could they? No one outside the family and Miss Levine knew. All they could possibly know was that Lady Violet was kept in the attic because it was what she wished.

"Come inside, and we'll settle you in," Miss Langley said. "Then all will be made clear. Won't it, Jack?"

She was a terrible liar. Not only was her apprehension written into every line on her forehead, but her voice pitched higher and higher with each word.

"You'll be treated with respect here," he said. "And you'll have every comfort."

"I had every comfort at Windamere," I said. "Respect too." Of sorts.

His mouth kicked up in a brief smile that was quickly dampened. "I see you like to argue."

"It appears to be the only course open to me. I tend to fight when I'm cornered."

"I know." He held up his hand. Three bloodied scratches raked down the back from knuckles to wrist.

"I'm—" *Sorry*, I'd been about to say. But I wouldn't apologize to my kidnapper for trying to save myself. "You ought to be more careful where you put your hands, Mr. Langley."

Again he gave that small smile, but once more it disappeared before taking proper hold. "Call me Jack. I'm not one for formalities."

"And you can call me Sylvia," Miss Langley said. "May we

call you Violet?"

"If you prefer." I peered past her to the house, a rather solid, dominating presence that looked as if it had been hewn from a mountain of rock. Yet it appealed to me in a way that Windamere never had. There was no symmetry to it, no evenness of form and certainly no beauty, but it was interesting, in a grim way.

"Welcome to Frakingham House," Sylvia said, following my gaze.

"You called it Freak House in the carriage."

"Did she now?" Jack glared at her from beneath a fringe of dark hair. He looked bedraggled, and I supposed I must have been equally unkempt. I touched my curls. *Ugh*. It was an untamed mess. I must have lost hat and hairpins somewhere along the way.

"That's what the villagers call it," Jack said. "Behind our backs."

"Behind *your* back perhaps," Sylvia said.

"Where are we?" I asked.

"A few hours from Windamere," Jack said. "Show her to her room, Syl, then come see us. I'll meet you there shortly."

"Where is 'there' exactly?" I asked. "And who else will I be meeting?"

Neither answered me. Sylvia steered me up the flagstone steps to an enormous arched doorway recessed deep into the stone moldings. Carved rosettes and a coat of arms decorated the lintel above.

Jack pushed open the door and allowed Sylvia and me to walk through first. As I passed him, a strange warmth spread along my veins to the tips of my fingers and toes. His breath hitched, but I didn't dare look at him. Didn't dare desire this man who'd kidnapped me.

I walked side by side with Sylvia to the grand staircase. It rose up to the first level then split in two with both sections continuing higher, disappearing through arched doors. Stone arches were everywhere. They formed the baluster, were carved into the walls to create niches, and enormous ones held up the vaulted roof. To my surprise, neither butler nor footman greeted us. If it had been Windamere, Pearson would have known we were about to walk through the front door before we did.

"Don't be afraid," Sylvia said with a squeeze of my arm.

"I'm not," I lied.

Our footfalls echoed throughout the cavernous space as we walked up the stairs and along a series of corridors that seemed to turn and turn again until I no longer knew whether I faced the front of the house or the back.

Sylvia stopped at a closed door. "This is your room."

"I'll never find my way out again. Or is that the point?"

"I see it'll take some time before you realize we're not going to harm you."

"You may not harm me, but you do intend to keep me prisoner here."

"This door will never be locked," she said, opening it. She said nothing about the front door and others leading outside, and I didn't ask. I suspect it would be something she wasn't allowed to discuss.

So who was forbidding her? The mysterious other person I was about to meet?

The bedroom was nothing at all like my attic one. Not only was it considerably larger and not covered in woolen hangings, but it was lavishly furnished. Paintings and tapestries hung on the walls, and the walls themselves were papered in a rich, deep burgundy. There was rather a lot of furniture, most of it beautifully made from dark wood, but it all looked comfortable, particularly the canopied bed with its swathes of crimson fabric covering the tester and cascading down the posts to form curtains.

"It's very grand," I said.

Sylvia fluffed up the cushion on one of the chairs. "We thought it appropriate for the daughter of an earl."

Would I be removed to the servants' quarters if they learned I was really plain Hannah Smith?

"It's a little chilly in here," she said. "Do you want the fire lit?"

"No. Don't trouble yourself."

The fireplace didn't look as if it had been lit in years. Perhaps it hadn't been. Perhaps I was the only visitor the room had ever seen. It did have the musty smell of a closed room, and the bedcovers and all the cushions looked crisp and new.

"Did you do these yourself?" I asked, indicating the embroidered cushions.

Sylvia smiled. "Yes. I painted most of the pictures too."

I studied the paintings. Some depicted ruins that resembled the ones I'd seen earlier, and others were of the lake or woods. They were a little dark and ethereal for my taste with stormy skies and an abundance of tangled vines, but they suited the house itself. "I hope you haven't removed them from your own room for me," I said.

"Oh no, I've done many more. They're in every room."

"You're very prolific."

"Oh, I meant every room that we inhabit. Most of Frakingham is empty. We don't need all of it."

"Who are 'we' exactly?"

She set the cushion down on the chair and arranged it just so, then rearranged it again. "Jack and me, of course, and Uncle August."

"Jack's father?"

"No."

"So he's Jack's uncle as well as yours?"

"Yes, of course. You do ask a lot of questions." She opened one of the cupboard doors. "There is a selection of gowns here, and jackets. They should all fit nicely as long as Jack was right."

I frowned. "Right about what?"

"Your measurements. He assured me he could tell your size just by looking at you."

"Jack first appeared at Windamere two weeks ago. Don't tell me you've had them all made since then based on the guess of someone who's only seen me a few times and at a distance?"

"Not all of them were made new. Some are altered ones of mine. I hope you don't mind. As to the fit...Jack's rarely wrong."

How irritating. "An expert on women's sizes, is he?"

She flashed me a mischievous grin. "I think you've made an impression on him. He almost smiled earlier, and when you get to know him better, you'll learn that he smiles rarely."

"I don't wish to get to know him. I wish to go home." It sounded petulant, but I didn't care. The Langley cousins might have been all solicitude toward me, but fear tightened my chest. Besides, I wanted to see Vi again. She must have been frantic with worry.

Sylvia turned suddenly and strode to the dressing table situated in the bay window. Her fingers lightly caressed the silver-capped perfume bottles, the combs, brushes and a silver candlestick and trinket boxes. It was as if she sought comfort in the familiar objects, or perhaps it was merely a way of avoiding eye contact with me. "You'll find unmentionables in the drawers."

I came up beside her and looked out the arch window. I could just see the lake and the ruins off to one side. Beyond that were wooded hills and little else. The village the cousins had spoken of must be in another direction. My soul thrilled at the sight of a new vista, so different from the one I had stared at every day for years. Yet I felt a stab of sorrow and the cold lump of unease too. I might never see the view over Windamere's park again.

"How old is this place?" I asked. Talking about the history of Frakingham might keep my nerves under control. Hopefully.

"The estate itself is ancient. People have been living and worshipping here for centuries." She pointed at the ruins. "That was Frakingham Abbey. It belonged to the Cistercian order, but was abandoned and fell into ruin around the time of the Dissolution of the Monasteries. It's rather a pleasant place to picnic now in the summertime."

"It looks eerie."

"I suppose it does." She looked at my crossed arms as I hugged myself. "Don't worry. There are no ghosts here that we know of. Indeed, this building is only about sixty years old, although you wouldn't know it."

"I thought it was medieval."

"Not at all. The previous Lord Frakingham wanted a grand house built in the Gothic style. He bankrupted the estate in the process, and his heir had to sell it when the place began to need repairs."

"Your uncle bought it?"

She tilted her chin and her eyes flashed. "He did. He's a self-made man, Uncle August. He worked his way up from nothing to be able to afford this. The son of a grocer now living in the same house that a lord built. Imagine that!"

"Yes, imagine." I had no idea how expensive it would be to buy something on the scale of Frakingham, but it must be considerable. Few Englishmen who hadn't been born into the upper echelons of society could afford it. No wonder Sylvia was proud of her uncle. "I'd like to meet him. Now, if you please." Commanding her allowed me to command my own trepidation as the full extent of my situation sank in. Well, to a certain extent at least.

Sylvia bristled. "Demands won't get you anywhere with Uncle. As it happens, he wants to see you immediately anyway. Let's get you ready." She spun me around and scanned me from head to toe. "These clothes are so drab. They won't do. Uncle August expects women of your status to dress accordingly. He likes order, you see." Her nimble fingers unbuttoned my jacket. "Servants ought to dress like servants, shopkeepers like shopkeepers and ladies like ladies. I'm surprised your father doesn't too. I'd have thought an earl would be more of a stickler for these things than Uncle."

"Who knows what Lord Wade thinks," I muttered as I allowed her to take off my jacket. There was no point in arguing with her, either about who my father may or may not be or about what I should wear to meet her uncle.

The prospect of meeting him filled me with foreboding. What sort of man inspired a nice girl like Sylvia to fumble nervously with the hooks and eyes on my dress? What sort of man had his niece and nephew kidnap for him?

CHAPTER 3

"Uncle August's rooms take up the entire top-most floor of the eastern wing of the house," Sylvia said as we hurried up the stairs. It was growing late in the day and being almost winter, the sun had already begun to set. The stairwell would have been dark if it wasn't for the small candle-shaped gas lamps attached to the walls. "There are a few things you ought to know about Uncle August before you meet him. First of all, he can't walk."

"How does he get about?"

"In a wheelchair."

"How did he lose the use of his legs?"

"It was an accident of some sort. He doesn't like to talk about it, and you're not to ask him."

That was like telling a fish not to swim. Yet I would hold my tongue, for now. My situation was too precarious to jeopardize it. "So he doesn't walk, but he lives all the way up here?" We'd reached the landing on the top floor. Sylvia had told me that the Langleys used only the eastern part of the house. Her uncle occupied the second floor, Sylvia, Jack and I had rooms on the first, and the ground floor was where the dining room could be found along with the formal drawing room and a more intimate informal parlor. Staff quarters were at the rear of the house with the kitchen and other service rooms.

"He has everything he needs up here," Sylvia said, her tone clipped.

"Everything except his freedom."

"When one doesn't have the use of one's legs, how much freedom can be expected?"

I thought it a narrow view, but didn't say so. Her curt manner invited no opinion. Besides, I was too anxious to argue with her. My stomach began to churn again and I had a pressing urge to turn around and run back down the stairs. I wondered what Sylvia and Jack would do if I just walked out the door.

Return to Windamere and kidnap the real Violet Jamieson?

We paused at a door on the landing, and Sylvia drew in a deep breath. She let it out slowly and knocked. The door was opened by Jack. He'd changed into formal evening wear of black tailcoat, waistcoat and trousers, white shirt and necktie. His hair was neatly combed back, and he looked every inch the lord of the manor. "Come in, ladies." He stepped aside. "He's waiting for you."

The room was very large, running half the length of the eastern wing. The far end was crowded with low tables, cupboards and desks, and a bench ran along one wall. Most of the surfaces were covered with lamps, paperwork or equipment that appeared to be scientific in nature. I recognized glass bottles, burners, at least two sets of scales and a cabinet housing dozens of small drawers. There were tools too, but I was too far away to identify them, and I probably couldn't anyway. Science was not my strength, as Miss Levine had frequently informed me.

The rest of the room where we stood was more sparsely furnished. A deep leather chair hunkered near the hearth, a small table close by, and one wall housed densely packed bookshelves. I couldn't make out their subject matter. Three of Sylvia's Frakingham paintings decorated another wall in a perfectly neat row. Not a single one hung crookedly.

There was another chair too, but it had wheels instead of legs and was occupied by a man dressed in a crimson and gold smoking jacket. He was quite handsome for a gentleman of about forty or so, despite the silvery streaks through his blond hair and the slight slackening of his jaw. He could have been even more handsome if he wasn't frowning so hard that his mouth was little more than a pink slash in his pale face. He was broad in the shoulders too, but his waistcoat bulged at his middle and he filled the chair completely.

Behind him stood a very tall man with stooped shoulders. His dark hair had receded, leaving a pronounced widow's peak at the front. It was difficult to tell how old he was, or what his nature might be. Indeed, he reminded me of an automaton awaiting his key to be turned. He simply stood there, quite still, his hands behind his back, staring unblinkingly ahead.

"Welcome, Lady Violet," the man in the wheelchair said. "I am August Langley. You've met my niece and nephew."

"You know I have," I snapped. I refused to make it easy for him, just as I refused to wipe my clammy palms down my skirt. Instead, I clasped my hands in front of me, the picture of calm serenity. Or so I hoped.

August Langley looked down at his lap and expelled a breath. It was a long, awkward moment before he spoke again. "Please sit down."

"I'd rather stand."

Sylvia gave a little gasp, and I felt Jack stiffen. It wasn't just that I didn't want to do this man's bidding—although that was certainly part of my reason for refusing—I also felt awkward sitting when others were standing. If Sylvia and Jack left, then perhaps I would sit to be on a level with Langley. Being alone with him was the very last thing I wanted, however.

"Forward, Bollard," Langley said.

As if his key had been turned, the man behind Langley

came to life. He stooped even more and pushed the wheelchair until Langley put up his hand to stop. The servant let the chair's handles go and settled once more into a stiff stance.

Langley tipped his head to look up at me. "I suppose you've guessed why you're here."

"Actually, no. It's quite a mystery. Your relations wouldn't divulge anything, despite my questions. After the method in which I was snatched from my home, I think I'm entitled to some answers, don't you?"

"Don't try to turn this into something it's not, Violet. I may call you Violet?"

I looked down my nose at him in the most imperial manner I could muster. It was not something I'd seen Vi ever do, even with Miss Levine, but I thought I made a good attempt. "What do you mean, turn it into something it's not? This is exactly what it appears to be. Abduction, imprisonment, extortion."

"Not extortion." He said nothing about the other two accusations. So it was true. He intended to...keep me.

My knees suddenly buckled, but Jack caught me by the elbow and steered me to the chair. I sat down heavily and struggled to catch my breath. The damned corset was too tight, and I had to gasp for air.

"It's not what you think," Jack said, crouching beside me. "We mean you no harm."

"Jack!" Langley snapped.

Jack straightened to his full height and glared down at his uncle with such ferocity I thought he might punch him. "She's frightened. I was the one who had to do your dirty work, and now she's frightened of *me*. Forgive me if I find the need to offer comfort."

Langley didn't take his hard gaze off his nephew, and I got the feeling if he could stand, he would square up to Jack and use his bulk to intimidate.

"Jack, perhaps now is not the time," Sylvia said in a sing-song voice. She came up beside him and looped her arm through his. Despite the placating tone of her voice, I could tell she was using all her strength to drag Jack away.

Finally, with a flare of his nostrils, Jack obliged her. I immediately felt less secure, and when I felt afraid, I talked.

"Then what do you want with me? If you mean me no harm, why am I here?"

Langley turned his steely gray gaze on me. "I'd heard you were clever."

I bristled. "Heard from whom?"

"Never mind that. You're here not because of *who* you are, but *what* you are."

My heartbeat slowed. My cheeks cooled. I sat very still and stared at Langley, although I didn't really see him. I'd known it all along, but I'd not wanted to admit it—I'd been kidnapped because they thought I was Vi, and Vi could start fires with her mind.

I swallowed hard. Langley was going to be in for a rude shock when he discovered I couldn't set anything alight without matches. And once he did, then what?

"But *why* do you want someone who can start fires?" I asked.

"To train you."

"Pardon?"

"Jack is going to teach you to use your power at will and control it."

I held up my hands, closed my eyes. My breath seemed unnaturally loud in my ears. "One thing at a time. For what purpose are you training me?"

"You cannot go about setting things ablaze willy nilly. You'll never be able to function in the real world if you don't learn to control it. We're going to help you, Violet. The sooner you see that, the sooner you'll accept your situation here."

"My situation being that I am a prisoner at Frakingham."

"Leaving would be foolish, and I've already established that you're a clever girl."

"Clever people can do foolish things."

He gave a slight nod. "I advise you against trying to leave. I know your father kept you confined to the attic, but you'll have more freedom here."

"He was worried I would set fire to something! And we lacked nothing."

"How do you know? Did you see what he gave your younger sister? Did you?"

His words would have hurt if I really were Lady Violet Jamieson. I knew she loved her father, despite everything. I think she secretly hoped he would remove her from the attic one day and introduce her to Society. She'd been bitterly disappointed after her eighteenth birthday when it became obvious her position, and mine, wouldn't change. She'd been sad—sadder—for weeks.

"That's enough, August," Jack said, his voice ominously low. "We don't want to rile her."

"Let's go downstairs," Sylvia said rather too brightly. "It must be almost dinnertime and I've a grand feast planned for our guest." She beamed at me so hard her cheeks must have ached from the effort.

"A good idea." Jack held out his hand to me, but quickly withdrew it with a glance in Langley's direction.

Langley scowled at him. "I believe Violet has one last question to ask me."

"I do," I said. "Why is Jack going to be the one to train me?"

"Do you care to answer this?" Langley pointed his chin at his nephew.

"Perhaps she shouldn't be overwhelmed just yet," Jack said.

"Come now. I know you're desperate to tell her."

"August. Don't. It's too soon."

"I'm ordering you to tell her!"

Jack stretched his fingers then closed them into fists. "Very well." He turned to me, and I was shocked at the feverish color of his green eyes, the mocking set of his mouth. "We're two of a kind, you and I, Lady Violet. As far as I know, we're the only two fire starters in England. Perhaps the world. I don't know why or 'ow, but we just is. We should join a travelin' sideshow. Or per'aps not travelin'. We could stay put. Make the customers come to us. Fleece 'em of every penny while we set their 'ats on fire."

"That's enough, Jack," Langley warned.

"Be famous, we would," Jack went on, his chest rising and falling with his hard breathing. "So what you fink, Vi?"

"I said, enough!"

"Jack," Sylvia whispered. She hesitantly reached for his hand, but when their fingers touched, she sprang back with a yelp. A spark shot from Jack's fingertip, but Sylvia stamped on it before it could scorch the rug.

I rose out of the chair and stared at Jack. I couldn't take my eyes off him. I'd never witnessed Vi during one of her episodes, my narcolepsy having shielded me from that, and to see actual sparks erupt from his bare skin was incredible. Not frightening, but...curiously thrilling.

It wasn't the only thing that shocked me. His outburst had been unexpected, but not nearly as much as his accent. It had changed from the cultured tones of a gentleman to something altogether different. Something I'd never heard before, but had read about in books. Indeed, some of the characters in Mr. Dickens' novels spoke like that in my head when I read their dialogue. It was only the poor characters, however—laborers, beggars, thieves, murderers and street urchins.

Which category did Jack Langley fit into?

"Are you all right?" Sylvia asked him.

Jack nodded without taking his gaze off me. He seemed calm, his face expressionless. It was his eyes that gave away his true feelings. They were as wild as a stormy sea, but just before he turned away, I caught a glimpse of something else in their depths. Something that made him look as lost as a little boy.

He strode out of the room, leaving the door open.

"Well." Sylvia huffed. "Is there anything else, Uncle?"

Langley lifted a hand in a dismissive gesture. "Jack knows what to do." He spoke heavily, as if the little scene had sapped his strength. "The window, Bollard."

The servant wheeled him toward the window and positioned the chair so that Langley could see out.

"Shall we dine, Violet?" Sylvia asked, smiling. Did she ever *not* smile?

I wanted to make a quip to prove that I was unaffected by everything I'd seen and heard, but nothing came to mind. I allowed Sylvia to lead me down the stairs to the dining room.

The long table was set for three, but the third place was empty. A footman brought in a soup tureen and set it on the sideboard. He hovered until Sylvia asked him to serve.

"Jack will come when he's ready," she said as the footman ladled soup into her bowl.

"His accent changed up there," I said. "Why is that?"

"It happens when he's...upset." She glanced at the door, then at the footman. He'd paused in his duties and stared at me. "You mustn't speak of it to him," she went on. "He doesn't like talking about it."

"First your uncle and his legs, and now Jack and his accent. Is there anything in this house that we can discuss?"

"The weather?" said Jack, striding in. He looked and sounded quite composed again. He sat at the vacant seat opposite us. "I'm starving. You must be too, Violet. We both missed our luncheon today." It seemed he was going to pretend nothing untoward had happened in his uncle's rooms.

"I'm not feeling particularly hungry." I waved away the second ladle of soup. "It's amazing what being abducted can do to one's appetite. I highly recommend it for ladies wishing to shrink their waists."

"Your waist is already tiny," Sylvia said.

"I think Violet was being sarcastic," Jack said.

"I know that. Forgive me if I'd prefer to gloss over the nastier events of the day while I'm eating."

"Speaking of which, I'm sorry to say that your reticule couldn't be saved, Syl."

"That's quite all right. I didn't like it anymore anyway." She suddenly brightened. "Perhaps we can go shopping together to buy a new one," she said to me. I was so taken aback that I spilled some soup on the tablecloth.

"I don't think that's a good idea," Jack said.

"But Uncle August told me she's free to come and go."

I witnessed a silent exchange between the cousins as they communicated without words. Jack's glare was quite stern, and Sylvia's smile changed from genuinely hopeful to falsely polite. She was not the sort who could hide her feelings.

"Perhaps we'll go when you've settled in," she said to me. "In a week or more."

"She won't have time before then anyway," Jack said. "Training begins tomorrow. I can't spare her."

"Ah yes, training," I said. "Your uncle stated that I was brought here so that you could help me learn to control my...affliction."

"It's not an affliction," Sylvia said. Her response sounded automatic, as if she were repeating something often said.

I grunted. "That's easy for you to say. As to the training, forgive me if I don't believe Mr. Langley."

Sylvia blinked her wide blue eyes. "Why wouldn't you believe him?"

"Because I was kidnapped."

"I don't understand."

"You knew I lived in the attic, which meant Lord Wade—my father—obviously cared little for me. It would also be a natural supposition that I was eager to leave the attic. My removal to your uncle's care could have gone ahead without this fuss if you'd simply *asked* to have me. All of which implies that your reasons are less pure, and you didn't wish to explain them to Lord Wade."

Sylvia continued to stare at me, her spoon drooping over her bowl, the soup forgotten.

"You make a lot of assumptions," Jack said.

"What does Langley really want with me?" I asked.

Jack returned to his soup, and it was left to Sylvia to answer. "Uncle August truly does want to help you." She glanced at Jack then back at me. "He's not a bad man."

I said nothing to that, and neither did Jack. The irony was, if they'd gone about the task as I'd suggested and asked Lord Wade's permission, they would have gotten the correct Violet Jamieson. As it was, they had an imposter. And this imposter was going to have to lie convincingly to make Jack believe she had the power to start fires.

Either that, or avoid lying altogether and simply escape.

CHAPTER 4

I slept more soundly than I'd expected. The mattress was so comfortable and the room so quiet that I didn't wake until mid-morning. I'd fleetingly thought about trying to escape before nodding off, but dismissed the idea almost instantly. It's what they'd expect me to do, and they'd be watching me far too closely the first night.

I rose and opened the heavy drapes, letting in the light. The sky was mostly blue with some high clouds scudding quickly across it thanks to what appeared to be a strong wind. The trees nearest the house swayed drunkenly, and two men who stood talking to one another in earnest held their hats on their heads. Or at least, one of them did. The other had a sturdy looking tall helmet. A military man?

It was odd that the two visitors were at the side of the house, not the front where they could be greeted. I briefly considered trying to catch their attention and begging their assistance in getting away from Frakingham, but it was likely they were friends of the Langleys and would be disinclined to believe me.

Besides, I wasn't appropriately dressed. I opened the cupboard and selected a simple morning dress of cream and green that fastened up the front. The cotton felt lovely and soft, and I spent a good minute or so just petting it and rubbing it against my cheek. It was perhaps a little flimsy for the cool weather, but I didn't care. It wasn't made of wool and that was all that mattered.

I dressed without a corset since I had no one to help and arranged my hair as best as I could. Without Vi, it was difficult to wrestle it all up into an elegant style, but I managed to pin some of it back so that I at least didn't look like a lion. I also found a silk choker in the same shade of green as the dress and fixed it around my throat.

Miracle of miracles, I found my way downstairs, only getting lost once and winding up at a locked door, which I assumed led to the disused part of the house. I found Sylvia in the small parlor looking out the window, her arms crossed as if hugging herself.

"Good morning," I said.

She turned and a smile quickly chased away her frown. "Good morning," she said, coming toward me. "Did you sleep well? I didn't want you woken until you were quite ready. You looked exhausted last night."

"Thank you. I slept like a log."

She studied me from head to toe, and her smile slipped a little. "You should have rung for one of the maids to help you dress."

"I...I'm not used to being dressed by a maid." Indeed, none of the Windamere attic rooms had been fitted with bell-pulls to summon the servants. They cleaned our bedroom when we were in the parlor, and they cleaned the parlor when we were in our bedroom or out walking. I rarely saw them and never rang for them.

"Really?" Sylvia looked quite shocked.

"My friend helped me and I helped her." An ache lodged in my heart at the thought of Vi, alone and sad in the attic. *Dear lord, take care of her. Don't let her fret too much.*

I must have looked quite forlorn because Sylvia took both my hands and gave them a squeeze. "Lucky you don't need a corset."

"I couldn't put it on by myself, and this dress was the only one with buttons down the front."

"It is a lovely dress and I hoped you'd like it, but it is more suited to warmer days."

"I'll be warm enough."

"Yes, of course." She tugged on the bell-pull near the fireplace. A small fire burned in the grate, but it was all the cozy room required. "You've missed breakfast, but I'll have Tommy fetch you something."

"Tommy?"

"The footman."

"You have only the one?"

"We live simply here and have no need of more. Uncle has Bollard to see to his needs, Tommy sees to ours, and there is the housekeeper, Mrs. Moore, two upstairs maids, the cook and a scullery maid. Oh, and Olson the carriageman who oversees the grooms. There are some gardeners too of course, but I don't know how many. Did you have much more at Windamere? I imagine you did, your father being the grand earl that he is."

"I don't know."

"Oh. No. Of course not." She cleared her throat and looked relieved when Tommy the footman entered. She requested a light breakfast be brought to me in the parlor, then indicated I should sit next to her on the settee. "Jack should be ready for you by the time you finish. Something unexpected has arisen this morning that required his attention. He's with Uncle now."

I didn't sit but went to the window instead. Nobody was about outside in the wind. "Does it have something to do with those visitors this morning?"

"You saw them?"

"Yes. Who were they?" I turned back to her, but she was looking down at an embroidery hoop in her lap. A sewing basket lay open at her feet. "Well?" I prompted.

"I'm not sure I'm at liberty to say." She picked up the hoop but didn't stitch. "Let's wait for Jack to arrive."

I was beginning to think Sylvia was very much like Vi. Neither wished to say or do the wrong thing, and both saw their position in the household as a lowly one compared to the other members. At least Sylvia put herself above the servants if her direct manner with Tommy was any indication. Vi had never given Miss Levine an order when she was perfectly within her rights to do so.

"I *will* take you shopping, you know," Sylvia said.

"Shopping?"

"After you've...settled in."

"I wouldn't hold out much hope. Your cousin doesn't want me to run off. Understandable considering the trouble he went to abducting me. I can't imagine how awful it must have been for him to pretend to be a gardener for two whole weeks."

"Is that sarcasm again?" Sylvia chuckled. "I dare you to say that to his face."

"Be careful. I rarely back down from a dare."

She dropped her needle, and her eyes widened. "It was only a joke. Don't tell him I suggested it."

"Why not? Are you afraid of him?"

She concentrated on her stitching for a long moment, then said, "He can be unpredictable."

Unpredictable. The word was like a siren song to me. I'd lived with routine and order my entire life. I did the same thing, day in and day out, saw the same people, walked the same paths. As much I would do anything to see Vi again, I was missing my life at Windamere less and less with each passing hour. Sylvia was different enough to be interesting, but her cousin was positively exciting. He was a mystery I wanted to solve. That morning, I'd looked for him around every corner, hoped to see him in every room I'd passed through.

"He never complained, you know," she said.

"Jack? About what?"

"About being a gardener. He only returned home once during that time, and all he spoke about was how poorly treated you were. It was he who discovered you were kept in the attic not of your own volition, but on Lord Wade's order."

"How could he possibly have learned that?"

"He said your governess tailed you everywhere on your walks, and that a free woman would not be in need of such close guard."

I was taken aback by this keen observation and rendered quite speechless.

Tommy arrived with my breakfast. I ate toast and poached eggs at the table by the window. Unlike the previous night, I was terribly hungry, and I was intent on finishing everything on my plate when Jack arrived.

"Good morning, ladies," he said. "Sleep well, Violet?"

My mouth was too full to respond in any manner other than a nod. I pressed a napkin to my lips to cover my chewing and to dab away any crumbs. It would be too embarrassing to have such a man as he see me with half my breakfast on my chin. He was too handsome, too self-assured, and I was the naive madwoman kept in an attic most of her life.

That didn't stop me from looking at him. It seemed that every time I set eyes on him, I noticed something new and intriguing. The intensity of his green eyes, the bow-like curve of his mouth, or the small scars on his upper lip and above his right eyebrow. With the sunlight streaming through the window, I saw that his hair had different shades of brown through it. Some light strands, some so dark to be almost black and everything in between.

"Yes, thank you," I finally said, sounding a little breathy.

"I'm afraid our training will have to wait. I must leave for Harborough immediately. I won't be back until this afternoon."

Sylvia set down her embroidery hoop. "Why?"

"August's business."

"Oh."

"Does it have anything to do with those men who were

here?" I asked.

"The constabulary?" Sylvia said.

"Police!"

Jack scowled at her. "Syl, hold your tongue."

"If you wish me to live here," I said, "then I expect to be treated as you treat each other. I won't be kept in the dark. Is that understood?"

Jack's eyes narrowed. "Quite," he bit off.

Sylvia made a small choking sound in the back of her throat, but when I glanced at her, she was intent on her embroidery.

"Were they both policemen?" I asked. "One wore a helmet."

"He was a constable in uniform," Jack said. "The plainly dressed gentleman was a detective inspector."

I set the napkin down and met those all-seeing green eyes. "Were they looking for me?"

"No." Was it my imagination, or did sympathy flicker across his face? "Someone broke in last night. Some of August's papers were stolen, and he's in a bit of a state about it. August in a state is not a pretty sight."

"What sort of papers?"

"I don't know. He wouldn't tell me. The inspector was called for this morning, and he and his constable asked some questions, took some notes and generally poked about. The only thing they achieved was making an inconvenience of themselves. They even failed to question all the staff, which means they missed a vital clue."

"What clue?"

"The imprint of a muddy boot was left on the floor in the scullery."

"How thrilling," Sylvia said. "Just like in a novel."

That earned another glare from Jack. "I measured it and sketched the sole pattern. I'll ride into Harborough to deliver it to the inspector."

"Are you certain the boot doesn't belong to one of the staff?"

"It was larger than mine or any of the staff."

To think, the authorities had been to Frakingham, and I'd missed them! I could have thrown myself upon their mercy and pleaded my case. Would they have taken my word over Langley's? I didn't know, but it galled that I had missed the opportunity to try.

"I'm sorry, Violet," Jack said. "I wanted to begin training today."

"Never mind." Another daring plan had already begun to form. I was desperate enough to carry it out too, despite the fear almost overriding my determination. Almost, but not quite.

"Just be sure not to have an episode in my absence. Or try to escape."

"I'll try not to, but alas I may not be able to control myself."

There was that twist of his mouth again, that almost smile. "Syl, will you be all right?"

"Of course."

"Tommy is here if you need anything."

I would have asked what he meant by that, but he excused himself and left. So I asked Sylvia instead. "Why did he mention Tommy?"

"I couldn't say."

"Is your footman going to restrain me if I try to leave?"

"Of course not."

I finished my breakfast and when I got up, she quickly rose too, toppling her embroidery hoop to the floor.

"I only wish to look out the window," I said. She sat again, her relief obvious.

I stood by the bay window and watched Jack ride down the drive on horseback. He was unaccompanied, which I thought a little unwise until I remembered he could set a man on fire if he found himself in trouble. He turned back suddenly as if he realized I'd been watching, and our gazes locked. He lifted his hand, and I thought he was about to wave, then he gathered up the reins again and turned away.

The horse broke into a gallop and Jack was soon gone from sight.

Now all I had to do was avoid Tommy and I would be free.

I waited until he had removed my breakfast dishes and been gone for some time before yawning. Sylvia didn't notice, so intent was she on her sewing. I yawned again and stretched.

"Still tired?" she said, looking up.

"I think I'll retreat to my room for a rest."

"Of course. I'll wake you for luncheon."

"I hope you don't mind, but I won't be joining you. Breakfast was quite sufficient to see me through the rest of the day."

Sylvia's face fell a little. "Oh. It'll just be me then."

I almost felt sorry for her, but her loneliness was not my concern. I left her and headed toward the staircase. Instead of going up, however, I walked straight past and through an arch that led to a short corridor and a number of closed doors. I bypassed those and headed along another corridor before reaching what appeared to be a door leading outside.

I glanced behind me. All silent. No one followed. I pushed the door open and found myself in an empty, graveled courtyard bordered on three sides by the house. I paused. Listened. Still nothing.

I half walked, half ran across the courtyard, looking left and right and back over my shoulder. The wind battered at my skirt and made a mockery of my attempt at arranging my own hair. By the time I'd exited the courtyard, my hair had broken free of its pins and whipped across my face as I glanced this way and that.

The benefit to finding myself at the rear of the house was that there was a wood nearby. Parks and formal gardens provided a pretty vista from the front and eastern side of Frakingham, but those open spaces weren't of much benefit for an escapee.

There was a graveled road and small grassy patch to cross

before I entered the safety of the trees. I checked once more behind me, then lifted my skirts and ran.

My heeled boots weren't made for running fast, but I didn't slow until I reached a dense clutch of trees that couldn't be seen from the wood's edge. I hid behind a large oak and leaned against the trunk to catch my breath.

Safe. No one had followed.

I pushed on, wanting to get far away from Frakingham and whatever the Langleys had in store for me. They might seem pleasant enough on the outside, but there was certainly something odd going on. Something besides Jack's ability to start fires. Perhaps if I really did have the same affliction as he, I would be more inclined to see if they really could help me control it, but I couldn't let them discover that I didn't and Vi did. I didn't trust them, and Vi was my one true friend, a sister in every sense of the word except biological. I would protect her with every last breath in my body.

To my sickening horror, I realized that meant I couldn't return to Windamere. The Langleys would look for me there. I had to steer them away from Vi and disappear forever.

Tears pricked my eyes, but I forced them back as I pushed on along a narrow, winding path. My mind and heart, however, remained in turmoil.

Perhaps that's why I didn't see Bollard until it was too late. He stepped out from behind a tree and grabbed my arm.

I screamed.

He clamped a hand over my mouth, dragging me back against his body. He smelled like damp earth and moldy leaves, and he carried a shovel. I struggled, but he was much too strong. I bit his hand.

He grunted and let go. I scampered away, but my heel was higher than what I was used to, and I toppled over and fell on my hands and knees in the decaying leaves. Bollard caught me again and shook the shovel in my face. His lips pulled back in a snarl. I turned my head and tried to jerk myself free, but his long fingers locked around my arm.

"Let me go!"

He shook his head but said nothing.

"I have a right to go where I please."

Another shake of his head. Why didn't he speak? Was the man a mute? No wonder the manor was dubbed Freak House. I was beginning to think Sylvia was the only normal one there, although even she had an excessively sunny disposition that didn't seem natural.

Bollard pulled me along with him back to the house. I resisted every step of the way, but of course it achieved nothing. It was like a bee flying into a gale—utterly pointless.

Bees could sting, though. When we reached the courtyard, I threw the most terrible, ear-splitting tantrum, complete with colorful curses and the most awful names I could think of to call him.

It didn't halt Bollard's progress in the least, but it did draw the attention of the servants and Sylvia. Three of the former peered out of the ground floor service windows as we passed, their eyes as wide as saucers. Sylvia burst out the same door I'd used to escape and ran across the courtyard to us. Her face was a picture of pale horror, her bottom lip quivering. She blinked back tears.

What she had to cry about, I'd no idea. I ought to be the one in tears. Yet I had no intention of crying, nor any inclination. The shouting must have got it all out of my system, and I quieted when Sylvia grabbed my other arm. She let it go again with a gasp.

"Be calm, Violet, for Heaven's sake!"

"I'm finding that rather difficult at the moment," I spat. "All things considered."

She edged away from me. "What happened? Violet, did you...?" She glanced up at the rooms on the top floor of the eastern wing, and a shiver wracked her. I followed her gaze and saw August Langley watching us from a window. "Did you try to escape?" she whispered.

I lifted my chin. "Of course. Unfortunately Bollard here was doing a bit of gardening in the woods. What *were* you doing, Bollard? Digging a grave?"

Sylvia gasped and covered her mouth with her hands. She eyed Bollard's shovel with horror.

Oh God, if she were frightened, then perhaps my off-handed remark wasn't so absurd.

Where before I'd felt hot from my exercise and anger, now icy cold fingers wrapped around my heart. I couldn't dislodge the notion from my head. But if he *was* digging a grave at his master's behest...whose was it?

Mine?

Bollard marched me to the house and up the stairs to Langley's rooms. Sylvia didn't follow.

"Aren't you coming?" I called back to her.

She shook her head. "I haven't been summoned."

I'd been right about her. That sunny disposition was all a façade. She was as afraid of her uncle as I was. I swallowed the lump in my throat. I could do this alone. There was nothing to fear. Indeed, I had every right to be furious, and damnation, I would be!

One look at the anger in Langley's eyes had my heart in my throat again and my nerves jangling. If he'd been able to stand and approach me, I'd no doubt he would have slapped me. He still might order Bollard to do it. The servant held his shovel like a weapon and stood between me and the door.

"Stupid, stupid girl," Langley spat. "I'd thought you more sensible than that."

"Then it seems you were quite wrong." Wrong about more things than he knew.

Color flushed his cheeks, but his lips turned stark white. "Did I give you permission to speak?"

As if being kept prisoner weren't enough, he wanted to make me as mute as Bollard too! "I don't need your permission, Mr. Langley," I snapped. "I have a tongue and will use it." Something inside me rose with my anger and filled me up until I was brimming with it. Something familiar yet wrong. Something terrible and ill-timed. My limbs became heavy, my mind dulled so that I could no longer form words. My skin felt like a thousand needles had been injected into it.

Langley's eyes widened. "*Move*, Bollard!" He wheeled himself away from me so fast he backed into the occasional table, knocking it over and sending the two books that had been open upon it to the floor. Bollard retreated to the door. To stop me from leaving?

It didn't matter. I knew what was about to happen, and I wouldn't be going anywhere.

The last thing I remembered was falling to the floor.

CHAPTER 5

I awoke as someone laid me gently on a bed. Bollard, I realized as I fought to lift my eyelids. It was my bed. The mute servant crossed the room and shut the curtains, then he left the room. The loud click of the door being locked was followed by complete silence. If I hadn't strictly been a prisoner before, I was now.

I was too exhausted to care.

I closed my eyes and lay on top of the bed. It felt strange not having Vi with me, caressing my hair until I returned to myself. It was pleasant not to wake to the smell of singed wool, however. As soon as I thought it, I wished I hadn't. No smoldering wool meant no Vi.

Would she be cured now that I wasn't there? She only ever started fires when I had a narcoleptic episode, so it was entirely possible that she would never have another one again now that I was gone.

Or would some other trigger take my place?

I blew out a breath and tried not to give into the overwhelming sadness. I did give into the tiredness that still dragged at my limbs, and I fell back to sleep

I awoke some time later with the strong sense that someone was watching me. It took my eyes a moment to adjust to the dim light, but when they did, I saw Jack sitting on a chair nearby.

He stiffened when he realized I was awake. "There's tea on the table beside the bed. It's probably gone cold by now."

I sat up and gratefully sipped the tea. It was indeed cold, but I didn't care. My mouth and throat were dry. I drained the cup and refilled it from the teapot.

"How do you feel?" he asked.

"Like a prisoner."

He leaned back in the chair and stretched out his long legs, crossing them at the ankles. He crossed his arms too and regarded me through half-lowered lashes. "August is furious that you tried to escape."

"He's not the only one with a temper."

"I can see that," he said with a sardonic tilt of his lips. "Why did you try to leave, Violet? I thought we went through this. I thought you understood that you would come to no harm here."

I swung my legs over the edge of the bed and sat up. "You'll forgive me if I don't believe a word you say. I find it hard to trust the man who kidnapped me. Even harder to trust the man who sits up there and makes it very clear I am not to question his authority or my predicament."

He rubbed a hand through his hair, upsetting its neat arrangement and causing it to tumble over his forehead. "I understand your need to know what's going on. Believe me, I do. But I can assure you, in this case, it's black and white. There are no secret experiments being conducted, no foul play."

I huffed out a humorless laugh. "If that's the case, why keep me against my will?"

"It doesn't have to be against your will, Violet." When I didn't answer, he added, "To protect you from yourself. And protect others too, of course."

There was a kernel of truth in what he said, although I still had strong doubts. "Then why the need to kidnap me from Windamere in the first place?"

The muscles in his jaw shifted and he looked away. It was a long time before he said, "That was necessary. Lord Wade would not have let you come to us freely, no matter what you think. He cared about you in his own way, but not enough to allow you to be trained. Like you, he would have suspected our reasons were more...insidious. It's unfortunate, but there's the truth of it."

I said nothing to that. I knew little of Lord Wade and nothing of his innermost thoughts toward his daughter.

"You can trust me, Violet. I give you my word on that."

I wanted so desperately to believe him. My heart ached with the need to trust him, to feel safe, to have a friend in this place. "Tell me, is my door still locked?"

"No."

I blinked at him. "When you leave here, will you lock it?"

"No. I've talked August into coming to an agreement."

"What sort of agreement?"

"It's conditional on an arrangement between you and me. If you agree not to try to escape, he'll allow you to go about the entire estate and into the village with Sylvia and I."

I cocked my head to the side and regarded him. "What makes you think I'll try not to escape even after promising not to?"

"Because I'm going to strike a deal with you. You may leave Frakingham by Christmas. You should be able to control your talent by then and will have no need of me anyway. I'll even drive you back and smooth things over with Lord Wade." He huffed out a breath. "Or try to."

It was a wonderful notion. Except for one major problem. "What if I make absolutely no progress by Christmas? Not even a little bit. Will you still let me go home?"

He shrugged. "Of course." By the dismissive way he said it, I got the feeling he didn't consider it an option.

"Then I agree to remain here until then." After all, Christmas was only five weeks away. I could pretend that my talent, as he called it, had gone into hibernation until then.

He gave a firm nod. "Good. I'm glad we could help each other out. Perhaps August won't want to rip my head off next time I walk into his rooms."

"He blames you for my attempted escape?"

"I was the one who convinced him you would stay once you realized we meant no harm." He gave me a lopsided smile. "It seems I didn't quite understand you as much as I thought I did."

"I'm glad to hear I'm not so predictable."

He stopped smiling. Indeed, his forehead creased into a frown. "You haven't asked how he is."

"Your uncle? Why should I? I assume he's still angry. Perhaps a little surprised too."

"You're right on both counts. Your unconsciousness was certainly unexpected. I'll go and talk to him again and tell him you've agreed to stay."

I made to rise, but he waved me back. "No, don't get up. Rest. If you don't mind, I'll send Sylvia in. She's been desperate to see you, but I made her wait."

"I'd like to see her too." I was startled to realize it was the truth. I didn't want to be alone. Sylvia's company would be a pleasant diversion.

Jack left and his cousin breezed past him as soon as he opened the door. She must have been waiting outside.

"Thank goodness you're all right!" She clasped my hands. "I was so worried about you when I realized you'd run away."

"You didn't even know I was gone until Bollard brought me back."

She glanced at the door and leaned closer to whisper. "Yes, well, I grew worried when I saw Bollard dragging you in and holding that shovel..." She shuddered and closed her eyes.

"Does he often go into the woods with gardening implements?"

"I don't think so. He rarely leaves Uncle's side. Uncle relies on him so much, not only to wheel him about, but he's also valet, laboratory assistant—"

"Laboratory assistant!"

"Oh yes. Uncle August may have sold his business interests, but he continues to dabble in this and that."

"This and that? Care to elaborate?"

"I would if I could, but I don't know what he does up there. Something pharmaceutical. It's all hocus pocus to me." She wiggled her fingers as if conjuring a rabbit from a hat.

"He's a chemist, your uncle? Is that how he made his money?"

"He's a microbiologist. He develops remedies, drugs, that sort of thing."

"Remedies for which ailments?"

"I forget now. Anyway, he and his partner sold a highly sought-after remedy to a large company for a lot of money. It allowed him to buy Frakingham. I was nine when we moved here."

"All three of you?"

She got up and walked to the window. "Both Jack's and my parents died when we were young. Uncle August took us in."

"They were brothers?"

"Who?"

"Your father, Jack's father, and your uncle. Otherwise you wouldn't all share the same surname."

"Yes. Of course they were brothers." She returned to looking out the window. I expected her to keep talking since she seemed to like the sound of her own voice, but she said nothing further.

"Is Bollard a genuine mute?" I asked.

She came back to sit on the bed beside me. "He's been that way for as long as I've known him."

"So he was born that way?"

She shrugged.

"Let me guess. Don't ask him?"

"Good lord, no!" She pressed a hand to her breast. "Please don't."

"He couldn't answer me even if I did." We both giggled but quickly stopped because it seemed a little cruel, although I wasn't sure Bollard deserved our sympathies. "Don't worry," I said. "I won't try to learn his secrets." The rest of the secrets harbored within Frakingham's walls were fair game, and I planned to uncover them before I left at Christmas.

Beginning with what Jack knew about his condition, and how he and Vi had come to be fire starters.

Sylvia suddenly hugged me so hard that I had to put out a hand to steady myself. "I'm so relieved you've agreed to accept your situation and stay," she said, blinking back tears. "It'll bring some peace and quiet to the house at last."

"Whatever do you mean?"

"I suppose you couldn't hear them from in here, but Jack and Uncle August argued over what to do with you as soon as Jack returned. Uncle wanted to keep you imprisoned in this room, but Jack refused to train you if that happened. Their voices became so loud I could hear them from downstairs. Uncle was still terribly upset by the break in, you see, and then your attempted escape and now this. He was most shaken."

"Jack didn't back down?"

"Oh no. He was most, uh, vehement in his response. I think Uncle grew quite afraid of him after his own temper cooled, and just gave in."

That surprised me, until I remembered what Jack was capable of doing if he chose to. I swallowed. It was a good reminder that Jack Langley was not to be crossed. If his own uncle feared what he'd do, then so must I.

"I'll have to remember to thank him," I said.

"I doubt he wants thanks for doing something he sees as right. He has the strongest morals, my cousin. Odd really, considering his past. Anyway." She clasped my hands in both of her own. "You and I will become great friends. I know it."

"It's only until Christmas." As soon as I said it, I wished I could take it back. Her face fell, her smile wobbled and finally slipped off altogether. Her hands retreated back to her lap.

"Oh. Of course." She stood and smoothed down the front of her skirt. "Only until Christmas."

"I hope there'll be many opportunities for us to go into the village together before then."

That seemed to appease her somewhat and her face lifted. "That's if Jack's training isn't so rigorous that he'll keep you all to himself."

The thought rather thrilled me, but I didn't think Sylvia needed to hear that.

**

Training began immediately after luncheon. Jack took me to a room on the first floor that had a horribly familiar furnishing arrangement. It was bare except for a table, two chairs and a lot of woolen rugs and hangings covering every inch of wood. Three pails of water stood near the fireplace as they did in every attic room at Windamere. It was the strangest thing to be in a similar room at another house that it quite took my breath away.

"I'm sorry it's not more comfortable," Jack said.

"That's all right. But why the caution here? My bedroom isn't set up like this, nor are the parlor or other rooms. You're not afraid I'll set those alight?"

"I didn't want you to suffer the indignity of stark conditions everywhere you went, so I told Sylvia we're not to upset you. If we appease you, then everything should be fine."

It was like listening to only half a conversation. "I don't understand. Appease me?"

"Keep you calm. Not make you angry." He looked at me askance. "You do understand what I'm saying, don't you? I know you can't control it, but you do realize that your talent is linked to your temper?"

I toyed with the idea of agreeing with him, and saying nothing, but I decided a little bit of the truth would lend credence to the lie I was living. "Are you saying that your ability to set things on fire comes about when you're angry?"

"Of course. But I can control my temper." He frowned. "Yours has a different trigger?"

"It's brought on by fear. Grave fear. For my loved ones." The choker at my throat suddenly felt too tight, and I stretched my neck, but it did little to relieve the constriction. I'd thought lying would be easy, but I suddenly felt as if Jack knew my every thought. Those green eyes drilled into me, and I eventually had to sit down and avoid his gaze altogether. If I hadn't, I may have found myself telling him everything.

"Jack, forgive me, but...you seem to know very little about this affliction," I said, rather boldly considering my weakened knees and racing heart.

"It's not an affliction. Don't ever call it that, Violet, or people will see you as a candidate for the asylum." He sat in the other chair without taking his eyes off me. "Fear, you say. Fear for your loved ones. But...that doesn't quite make sense. Firstly, I thought you had no loved ones at Windamere."

"I had a companion."

He nodded slowly. "I saw her with you on your walks. Hannah Smith, isn't it?"

Hearing him say my name for the first time shook me to the core. "You've not answered my question," I said.

"You're right. I know only my own case. I'd assumed yours was exactly the same."

"How did you—we—get this way?"

He shrugged. "I don't know. I've been like this for as long as I can remember, so I suppose I was born with it. You?"

"The same. Do you know anyone else who can set things alight?"

"No." He shook his head slowly. "I admit I don't understand why it's only you and I."

"How did you become aware that Lady Violet Jamieson was like you? Considering I've been locked away for so long, it could hardly have been local gossip. Not even the servants knew."

"Are you sure they didn't? If you had servants attending your rooms at all, then they would have seen the burn marks and formed a conclusion of their own."

"Yes, but the *right* conclusion? That is rather a big leap to take, don't you think?"

Another shrug, but he made no further comment.

"So was it gossip that made you aware of me?"

His gaze shifted away. "August told me about you."

"Your uncle? How did he learn of my existence?"

"I don't know. He wouldn't say."

"I see. *When* did he tell you?"

A brief smile touched his lips. "The day before I came to Windamere as a new gardener. I couldn't start quickly enough once I heard."

"You were that eager to spy on me?"

"Of course. I thought I was the only one like this. I thought I was alone." He raised his gaze to mine, and heat shimmered down my body all the way to my toes. "Do you know how relieved I was to find out about you? How happy?" He gave me a grim smile. "Yes, I suppose you do."

My breath came in shallow bursts so that my next words came out as a whisper. "But you weren't alone. You had your uncle and Sylvia."

"It's not the same."

"Isn't it?" I was genuinely curious. Is that how Vi felt? All alone despite having me for company? It explained her melancholy and all those forlorn gazes out the window.

"Not nearly the same." His murmur vibrated through me. He spoke as if I were the only person in the entire world who could ever understand him, and that was a heady, thrilling thing. To be cherished by such an enigmatic, handsome man would make any woman giddy.

I could not let it affect me. I was all too aware that I was not the one who understood him. It was Vi. She deserved his attentions, not me. I felt quite terrible that I was responsible for keeping them apart, in a way, yet I felt even more terrible at the jealousy brewing inside me. A very big part of me wanted to keep this man to myself.

"So," I said in an attempt to shatter the thick silence that had enveloped us. "You said your uncle told you about me."

"He did." He shifted in the chair, stretching out his long legs to the side, away from me. The movement did indeed break the last remaining strain of tension, but it was unfortunately replaced with awkwardness.

"It's odd that you and I live in the same county as one another," I said.

"Is it?"

"And that there are none others like us in all of England."

"Isn't there? There may be, but we may not be aware of them yet."

"Surely you would have heard."

"I'd not heard of you two weeks ago."

"Your uncle had."

He lifted one shoulder. "I'd wager there are a great many things in this world that exist, but nobody knows about them."

"Like what?"

"Spirits, for one thing."

"Ghosts?" I scoffed. "Don't be ridiculous. Ghosts don't exist."

"If you say so." He stood suddenly. "We ought to begin."

"I have more questions."

"I thought you might." He winked. "Try saving them until later when we have more time."

"But I'd like to ask them now."

"Lady Violet, I do believe you're stalling."

I crossed my arms and tried not to let him see that he was right. "Very well. Let's begin. What should I do?"

He put his hands on his hips and studied me. "We begin with *you* answering some questions. I need to understand your talent better. If there are more differences between us than the trigger then I may need to change my methods. Tell me, where do you feel hottest?"

"Whatever do you mean?"

"Your fingers, your feet, or inside you?"

"I don't know. I've never really thought about it."

"Think about it now."

I shrugged. "I couldn't really say right now."

"Do you feel it coming on?"

"Coming on?"

"Like a wave, a surge through your body."

"Yes," I lied. I thought it best to agree with his own symptoms since Vi had never confided in me about hers.

"And you can't stop it from bursting out of you?"

"You already know I can't."

"Have you ever tried?"

"Tried?"

"Have you tried to control your fear? For me, it's a matter of dampening my temper, but for you, it'll be overcoming your fear since that's what you think is your trigger. You could try breathing exercises or counting backwards whenever you feel scared."

"I can't say I've ever tried to quell my fears like that."

"Shall we attempt to now?"

"Counting backwards? You're beginning to sound like Miss Levine. Will I receive a rap across the knuckles if I falter?"

"Will that induce enough fear to set off the sparks?"

I gave him a withering glare, and he gave me that now familiar almost-smile.

"You're right," he said. "There's no point in doing breathing exercises if we don't first study how it's triggered."

"Are you going to leap out from behind a cupboard and shout 'Boo'?"

He didn't even laugh at that, although I couldn't help smirking. I'd be checking around corners for the next five weeks.

"You don't strike me as the fearful sort." He continued to look at me, twisting his mouth in thought as he studied me.

"It's very odd that your talent would be triggered in that manner when it's not something you appear to suffer from overmuch. Besides, you must have been afraid when I abducted you, yet nothing happened."

"You drugged me! And anyway, how do you know it's odd? For all we know, you may be the odd one and everyone else with our afflic—talent—has the same trigger as me."

"You may be right. The question still stands—how am I going to frighten you?"

"You could get Bollard to chase me with a shovel again." My joke fell flat, and I shuddered at the memory of stumbling across the mute in the woods.

Jack was at my side in an instant. He touched my hands, and sparks zapped between us. I felt a shock through to my bones. It was as if every part of me had been struck by lightning and even after he drew back, my nerves continued to sizzle.

He stood and shook out his hands. "Bloody hell," he muttered. "I'm sorry. Are you all right?"

I expected to see burns on his hands, but they appeared perfectly fine. As did mine. They did, however, feel hot. Indeed, I felt hot all over. I removed the choker from around my neck, but it did little to alleviate my discomfort.

"Why did that happen?" I asked. "I thought you only started fires when you were angry."

He lifted one shoulder in a shrug and turned away.

"You touched me when you kidnapped me, yet that didn't happen," I said, talking more to myself than him. I didn't expect an explanation and nor did he offer one.

He made a great fuss with the pails, kicking them gently and watching the water ripple on the surface.

I studied my palms again. They were still hot, as was the rest of me, but they no longer tingled. Remarkable. "There seems to be so much that we don't know about this. Jack, I must ask...what makes you think I can be trained at all?"

He stopped kicking the buckets and knelt on one knee in front of me. There was resignation in his eyes, and a deep sadness, but I did not touch him like I wanted to. "We have to try, Violet." His voice was smooth and chocolaty thick. Despite my confusion and uncertainty, it instantly lifted my spirits. "Otherwise you'll be a prisoner for the rest of your life. Now." He stood again and removed his waistcoat and rolled up his sleeves.

"Jack!" I shielded my eyes with my hand, but peeked through the fingers. "I may have lived a sheltered life, but I do know undressing in company is not appropriate."

"To hell with propriety. I'm boiling inside."

I quite understood, and I thanked God that I wasn't wearing a corset and had chosen a light dress for the day. "If you're trying to frighten me, it's not working."

He laughed. "I'm not trying to frighten you. Not yet. Let's begin with some breathing exercises you can employ for when you're feeling afraid."

***

I couldn't sleep that night. Thoughts of Jack whirled through my head. I couldn't block them out, nor did I want to. I liked how he looked at me. I liked how he made me feel. Except when he zapped me, that is. It had taken the rest of the day before my body cooled enough to feel comfortable again. Indeed, I was still a little warm, so I rose to open the window. The air was cold but didn't alleviate the heat throbbing through me. Jack's touch had indeed been powerful, and the effects long-lasting.

Voices drifted up to me from below. In the moonlight, I could just make out two figures standing side by side. One wore a long overcoat and hat. The other did not. Both had the stance and size of men.

"He'll be in a lot of trouble if Langley finds out," said a voice I instantly recognized as Jack's. Why was he referring to his uncle by his surname?

"We don't know it's 'im." Good lord, it was Tommy, speaking in a slum accent similar to what I'd heard Jack use that one time in Langley's rooms. His tones had been cultured earlier as befitted a footman in a grand house, so why the slip now?

I leaned further out the window to hear more.

"Of course it's him," Jack said. "The maid said—"

"She 'as a name, Jack. Maud. You mighta risen up 'igh now, but you better not f'get where you came from. Wouldna want that pretty lady knowin' what you really is, would ya?"

Something flared in the darkness, and I realized with a start that it was Jack's fingers. There were no sparks, but they did glow.

"Jesus bloody Christ, Jack-o'-lantern!" Tommy backed away. "I don' mean no 'arm. I won' tell 'er nuffin'. Put yer 'ands away."

The glow went out. "*Maud* said the intruder she saw was a tall man with a big nose and a scar across one eye. Unless you know of another fitting that description, then I'd wager it was Patrick."

"But Patrick's in London with the others."

"It would seem he's made at least one trip into the country recently. I'll go to London and warn him to keep low."

"What? You not gonna let the Bobbies deal wiv 'im? My, my, seems you ain't f'got us after all."

"Of course I haven't forgotten you, you know that. You're my family. Always have been, always will be." Jack gave Tommy a slap on the back, and Tommy briefly clasped Jack's arm.

"You got anuvver family now," Tommy said. "An uncle and a cousin. Don' fink they'd like 'earin' you talk about the likes o' Patrick and me as closer to you than them."

Jack tipped his head back as if he were about to look up. I ducked inside and flattened myself against the wall. My heart thundered in my chest and I closed my eyes, held my breath.

"They're not my family," I heard Jack say, and I breathed out again. It would appear he hadn't seen me.

"Aye. No need to feel bad about what Patrick stole then,

is it? Langley's just anuvver toff." The gravel crunched beneath their boots as the two men walked away.

I breathed deeply several times. I still couldn't believe what I'd just heard, yet I must. Jack not only knew the thief, he was protecting him.

They're not my family, he'd said. If that were the case, why was he living at Frakingham House at all?

To fleece Langley of his wealth by pretending to be his nephew? Or was there something more sinister going on?

CHAPTER 6

"Try focusing inward," said Jack.

"How do I do that?" I sat in the training room with my eyes shut. When Jack had asked me to close them I'd thought he was going to frighten me in some way, but he hadn't.

"Try to imagine your insides," he said.

I pulled a face. "Do I have to?"

"Not your innards, but the flow of energy. Your essence, if you like." He must have been circling my chair because his voice sounded like it was surrounding me. I felt completely immersed in its rich honey-thick tones. "Can you feel it, Violet? The flow of heat beneath your skin, the quiet thump of warm blood through your veins."

My breath came in short bursts, and I had to fight for every one. I could only manage a nod, but I couldn't explain that what I felt was perhaps as a result of his close proximity and the lilt of his voice. Heat did indeed swell inside me.

I opened my eyes and stood up, almost bumping into him. He managed to back away just in time.

"What's wrong?" he asked.

I put a hand to my forehead. "I'm tired. This has been an exhausting day and I didn't—" I was about to tell him I hadn't slept well, but I didn't want to plant the suspicion that I'd overheard his conversation with Tommy. "I didn't think we'd be training all morning."

"Would you prefer to sit and embroider with Sylvia?"

"Actually, I would. Perhaps we can resume later?"

He frowned. "Are you sure you're all right? You do look tired."

"I'm fine," I said brightly. "But all this anatomical talk is quite overwhelming. My poor head can't cope."

His gaze narrowed. "You seemed to comprehend it well enough. Did you have a tutor?"

"Four. They each came regularly, but never at the same time."

"I saw them. I'd assumed they were there to teach your sister."

"Perhaps they did. I don't know. It was Mr. Upworth who taught us about biology of plants and animals. Humans weren't included in our education, thankfully."

"The basic structure is the same between many animals and humans."

"Oh?"

"Don't look so horrified. I haven't cut up dead bodies to discover that fact. Like you, I had tutors. And books."

"The only books I've seen are in your uncle's rooms."

"And those are the ones I read. He's generous when it comes to their use. He says knowledge is the only way for a man to rise above the class in which he was born. You should ask to borrow something when you get bored with embroidery."

"No thank you. I think it's best that I avoid Mr. Langley for a while."

"He won't be mad at you anymore. Trust me, he's quick to anger and just as quick to forgive, although perhaps not forget. Not entirely," he muttered.

"I thought you didn't like him."

"We have our differences, but he's been...generous to me. And to Sylvia."

"So he should be. He is your uncle." I was fishing for more information about their relationship, but if he detected it, he didn't give any indication. "Why don't you call him Uncle August like Sylvia does?"

"It's what we both prefer. So you're back to being suspicious again, are you?"

"No!"

"Then why all the questions? I thought you got them out of your system yesterday."

I waved my hand and turned to the door. I didn't think I could lie to him while looking him in the eye. He'd surely know.

"Are you going to the parlor to see Sylvia?" he asked.

I paused in the doorway and blinked back at him. "Worried I'll try to escape again?"

"No, I just want to know where I can find you when it's time to resume training."

I groaned. "We're not finished for the day?"

"Not even close."

"Then I look forward to seeing you again."

"No, you don't, but I appreciate your attempt at flattery anyway."

In truth, I *did* look forward to seeing him again, but it was far less humiliating to laugh than tell him that.

***

While it was pleasant enough embroidering and listening to Sylvia's chatter, I soon found myself looking up at every sound, hoping Jack would enter the parlor. Just as a watched pot never boils, a watched door never opens, except to let in the footman. He came to deliver a letter to Sylvia. As he was about to leave, I set aside my embroidery and followed him.

"Tommy, wait a moment."

"Yes, my lady?" While his accent wasn't as cultured as Jack's, there was little hint of the speech pattern he'd used the night before when I'd overheard their conversation. It would seem they could both switch seamlessly from one accent to the other.

"Is Mr. Jack Langley about?" I asked.

"I believe he went to the lake."

"The lake? Whatever for?"

"For a...walk."

His hesitation intrigued me. "Thank you, Tommy." He left and I returned to the parlor. Sylvia was reading her letter and didn't look up. "Do you mind if I go for a stroll to the lake?"

She dropped the letter to her lap. "I...I suppose not." She nibbled her lower lip, clearly considering whether she ought to let me go. "You won't forget your agreement."

"No, but if it makes you feel any better, you may watch me from the window and have Tommy escort me."

"There's no need for an escort." She said nothing about not watching. Indeed, she rose from the sofa as I left and settled onto the window seat with her correspondence.

I waved to her once I was outside and she waved back, then pretended to read her letter when she actually watched me from behind her lowered lashes. I crossed the drive and lawn and walked to the lake.

It was a starkly beautiful place. Weeping willows hunched over the bank like tired ghosts, their bare branches drooping into the sleek, dark water. The grass was a green so bright it almost hurt to look at it, although it was muddy in patches, particularly on the banks of the lake itself. The vista would be lovely covered with snow. Hopefully there'd be some by Christmas. I'd like to see it.

I wondered if Tommy was mistaken because I didn't see any sign of Jack at the lake. Not at first. Then movement on the far bank caught my attention. He was running between three trees, touching each trunk, then repeating the course over and over. He was lightning fast. He reached each tree in a fraction of the time it would have taken me.

When he finally finished running, he climbed one of the trees and walked along a horizontal branch. He didn't hold onto any of the other branches, but kept his arms outstretched for balance. He walked up and back several times, then stopped in the middle and jumped off. He caught the branch with both hands and pulled himself up until his chin was above it, then lowered himself again. He repeated the exercise, varying the speeds until finally he let go and landed deftly on the ground.

I was about to call out and wave when he did a most unexpected thing. He walked to the lake's edge and kept going. Good lord, he was having a dip! I know he didn't feel the cold, but it was late November! Madness.

He swam toward me, making it look easy. I'd never swum before, never even *seen* anyone swim, and I couldn't look away. He slipped across the surface like a boat, his strokes effortless, graceful. Perhaps I should have left and not let him know I'd been watching, but I was too intrigued. That a man could be as natural in the water as out of it was amazing.

I thought he hadn't noticed me, so when he stood up a few feet from the edge and acknowledged me with a nod, I was taken aback. I blushed fiercely and looked away. He wore only a sodden shirt and breeches, and both clung to him like skin, outlining the muscular contours of his chest, shoulders and thighs. He possessed an athletic build, tall and broad across the shoulders, tapering to a narrow waist. Magnificent. Better than any classical statue depicted in Vi's copy of *Gods of the Ancient World*.

"Grew bored with embroidery, did you?" he asked, wading through the shallows toward me. Water cascaded off his body and dripped from his hair and lashes. The corners of his mouth lifted in a teasing smile. He looked like a devilish sprite, up to no good.

"I, um..." It was all I could manage in my addled state.

"Something the matter with your tongue? And here I thought you weren't afraid to speak your mind."

Damn him. He knew the effect he had on me. Not only did my face feel like it was on fire, but I couldn't think of anything witty to say to dispel my humiliation. All I could do was turn away, but it was too late. I'd already seen much more than I'd ever seen of a man before.

I liked it.

"Shall we walk back to the house together," he said. "Or would Sylvia have a fit if she knew you'd seen me like this?"

"She didn't know you were here when I said I was going for a walk to the lake."

"In that case, perhaps we should return separately. I see no need to endure a lecture from my little cousin on propriety."

"It bothers her that much?"

"It doesn't bother you? You are the sheltered one after all."

Determined not to let him know how affected I was by his state, I turned round to look at him, keeping my face as blank as I could. "It doesn't *bother* me, no. We could chalk the experience up to training if you like. After all, I feel quite...enlightened." Light-headed more like. My gaze dipped to his groin. The tight, wet breeches left nothing to the imagination, and to my dismay, my face heated to the very tips of my ears again.

Even worse, Jack looked amused at my discomfort. "Glad to be of service in furthering your education," he said. "Shall I escort you back to Sylvia's lecture hall?"

"Shouldn't you change first?"

"I'll change back at the house."

"Didn't you bring spare clothes with you? Shoes?"

"Have you ever put wet feet into shoes? It's not exactly comfortable."

I didn't suggest that he should have had the foresight to bring a towel to dry himself. "You're not cold?"

"I never get cold."

"Oh. Right. Of course not. So what were you doing on the other side of the lake just now?"

"You saw that?" He walked off, not waiting for my answer, or for me for that matter. Although he wore no shoes, he wasn't careful where he set his feet. Dirt and stones didn't seem to trouble him. "I was exercising. It helps me think."

I hurried to catch up. "What were you thinking about?"

"You don't want to know."

"Actually, I do."

"Let me put it another way. I don't want to tell you, Violet."

"Very well. Shall we talk about more inane things then? Something you *do* want to talk about?"

"If you wish."

His evasiveness grated. So much so that all I could think about was digging further to find some answers. "You were very fast over there."

"I thought we were going to talk about dull things."

"You're assuming I find you interesting."

I thought I heard him chuckle, but there was no sign of amusement on his face. "You wound me, Violet."

"Somehow I doubt that." I couldn't help laughing. I certainly did not find him dull, and he knew it. That didn't mean I was going to let him distract me from my mission. "Where did you learn to be so fast? And how did you learn to swim? Was it before or after you came to live here?"

"It's something I've always known how to do. I was never taught."

Never taught? Surely swimming was a difficult activity to master. Unless he were a fish, how could he possibly just 'know how' to do it? "Like the fire starting," I muttered.

He stopped. Looked at me. "You may be onto something. Perhaps they're linked. I never considered it before. Can *you* swim?"

"I've never tried."

"Perhaps you should."

"Jack, I am *not* going into the lake."

Crinkles appeared at the corners of his eyes. "Pity." He glanced up at the top floor of the house, and I followed his gaze. I expected to see Langley looking down at us, but instead it was Bollard's emotionless face that peered from the window. "I need to see August about something," Jack said. "I'll see you later."

"You're not going to suggest to him that I go swimming I hope. Because if you do, I shall have to break our agreement and escape."

"Come now. Where's that spirit I've witnessed countless times?"

"Hiding from you and your schemes."

"I wouldn't let you drown." His eyes danced merrily. "Perhaps only a dunking or two. I do owe you after you gave me a reticule full of vomit."

"The vomit and the scratches on your hands are nothing compared to what I'll do if you suggest I go swimming in the lake."

"Don't worry. As amusing as it would be to see you swimming, what I have in mind is much more interesting."

"Oh? What is it?"

"Let me speak to my uncle first." He nodded at the parlor window on the first floor. Sylvia glared at us, her arms crossed, her fingers tapping on her sleeve. "You'd better go inside and receive your lecture."

"*My* lecture! You're the half-naked wet one. I'm an innocent who's led a sheltered life, remember?" I turned to go into the house, but not before I saw something that sent a thrill of tingles down my spine. Jack actually grinned.

***

Jack didn't join us until after luncheon. He'd been gone a long time considering all he had to do was change and speak to his uncle. Perhaps they were arguing again. Sylvia must have had the same thought because she kept glancing at the door then frowning when nobody walked through it. Her concerns didn't stop her tongue, however. She chatted the entire time, gossiping about neighbors I'd not yet met.

We were both relieved when Jack finally came into the parlor.

"Well?" Sylvia said before he'd taken two steps inside. "Why did you need to speak to Uncle August?"

"I see you've been talking about me again."

Sylvia clicked her tongue. "Honestly, Jack, you're not *that* interesting."

He pressed a hand to his heart. "You wound me, dear cousin." He seemed in very good spirits, the best I'd seen him in since my arrival at Frakingham.

Sylvia must have noticed it too because she eyed him warily. "Surely you've not just come from Uncle's rooms. You're much too cheerful."

"I was with August for only a few minutes, then I went to see Olson in the stables."

"You've been in the stables the entire time?" I asked.

"I like to help out with the horses on occasion."

Sylvia sniffed. "I think it's cruel not to come here immediately when you've got news you knew we'd be waiting to hear."

"How do you know it's something for your ears? It could be nothing to do with either of you."

"Just tell us!"

He held up his hands. "Very well. We're going to London."

I don't know who gasped loudest, Sylvia or me. She certainly recovered from the shock first. "London? All three of us?"

"Yes."

"And Uncle has agreed?" Her gaze slid to me then away again.

"Yes."

"He trusts I won't try to escape?" I asked. It was quite unbelievable. There had to be something else he wasn't telling us.

"We have an agreement, Violet. I've assured him you'll keep your word and not try to escape. You've proved that already when you came to the lake."

"Her behavior was perfect," Sylvia agreed. "Unlike yours, Cousin. Did you *have* to parade about like that? It was terribly vulgar."

"So why are we three going to London at all?" I asked to

73

diffuse their argument. "Does it have something to do with my training?"

He nodded. "You're going to see a hypnotist."

"A hypnotist!" Sylvia cried.

"Whatever for?" I asked.

"I think something is blocking your talent. A barrier of some sort, mental not physical. I have a theory that if we remove the barrier, you'll have better access to the fire within you, and better access will mean you can summon it at will. Or dampen it, if need be."

"Can a hypnotist remove the blockage?"

"I hope so. We won't know until he looks at you. August knows of a fellow in London and agreed it's a good idea for you to see him. He's given me a letter of introduction, and we'll leave early tomorrow morning. We'll be in London by late afternoon and can see him the following day."

"Do you think the appointment will take long?" Sylvia asked.

"Why?"

"We simply *must* go shopping. I'm not traveling all that way and not visiting Oxford Street."

Jack's eyes softened. "We'll certainly have time for shopping. Indeed, I can hardly wait. I live to carry your purchases up and down Oxford Street."

"Don't be silly. Tommy can carry the boxes to the carriage. You won't need to do a thing except pay. Just think—we're going to *London*. How thrilling."

"I've read about it," I said. "It's seems like an exciting place."

"Exciting is not a word I choose to associate with London," Jack muttered, his good humor having slipped away.

Sylvia sucked in her top lip. "No, of course you wouldn't."

I lifted my brow in inquiry, but either she didn't notice or chose to ignore me. "You've been to London before?" I asked Jack.

He hesitated then said, "Yes."

"Many times?"

"Yes. Violet, would you care to go riding with me this afternoon?"

It took me a moment to follow the abrupt shift in conversation. I wanted to ask him more about London, but he seemed to want to avoid a discussion on the subject. "Riding? On a horse?"

"That's usually how riding is done."

"But I've never been on a horse before." To tell the truth, I was a little frightened of the creatures.

"Then it's about time you learned."

"Wait a moment," said Sylvia, holding up a hand. "I'll have to come. To chaperone," she added when both Jack and I stared at her. "You shouldn't be alone together."

"For God's sake, Syl. I've been alone with her all morning in a room with the door closed and then again down at the lake."

"That was different. The room was work, and I didn't know you were at the lake. If I had, I would've escorted her. You can't go gallivanting around the estate together where anybody could see. I won't allow it, and I doubt Uncle would either."

"I'm not sure August cares one way or another."

"He should. If he wants to fit in with Society then he must follow the rules."

"Just because he has this house doesn't mean he wants to fit into Society. You know how he hates that class of people."

Sylvia's gaze once more flicked to me and she blushed ever so slightly and looked away. I supposed they considered me part of 'that class of people.' If only they knew—I was far beneath them both on the social ladder.

"Nevertheless," she said. "I ought to chaperone you."

Jack sighed. "Very well. I'll wait for you both in the stables."

Twenty minutes later, I entered the stables without Sylvia.

"She's not coming after all," I told Jack when he asked. "She took one step outside and decided it was much too cold. It appears she cares more for her comfort than my reputation."

This last was said as a joke, but Jack didn't even smile. "I suppose it would be cold for her out here," he said.

"I admit I thought about staying inside too."

"You're cold?"

"Afraid. The closest I've ever been to a horse was the other day in the carriage."

"You'll be fine. Clover is our oldest nag. She can barely raise a trot." He indicated I should walk into the stables ahead of him. "There have been a lot of firsts for you in the last few days, haven't there?" he said, taking a saddle from one of the grooms.

"My first time in a carriage," I said. "First time wearing something that isn't woolen, first time sleeping in a room on my own." First time alone with a man.

I watched as he saddled his horse. He wore no jacket or coat, and I could clearly see the muscles flex beneath his shirt.

"Then it's my duty to make this inaugural ride a pleasant experience," he said, suddenly turning and catching me staring.

I mumbled something, I hardly knew what. He turned back to his task, but not before I saw how pink his cheeks had become.

He and the groom finished saddling the horses and led them outside. Jack paused to remove a black riding jacket hanging from a hook and put it on. He cut quite the gentlemanly figure in it with buff riding breeches and black boots. I had difficulty concentrating as he explained how to mount, and I ended up gratefully accepting the assistance of the groom. I managed it the first time, but only because Clover remained perfectly still. If she'd pranced about like Jack's horse, I would have surely fallen off the other side.

"She'll just follow along," Jack said, urging his horse forward. "You won't have to do a thing."

Clover did indeed meekly follow his horse, but that didn't stop me from clutching the reins so tightly that my fingers ached by the time we reached the lake.

"Relax a little," Jack said, his voice clear in the breathless quiet. "You're doing well."

"I must look awkward."

"Not at all. You look elegant."

I snorted. "Thanks to this riding habit. Sylvia has exquisite taste and seems to have been well versed in my size and coloring before my arrival. I believe I have you to thank for that."

"I can assure you, it's not just the clothes. You've got a natural gift for riding. It's a shame Lord Wade never allowed you and Miss Smith to learn."

"I suggested it to her once, but she was much too frightened by the idea so I never pursued the matter."

"A shame. Could you not have gone without her? Your governess could have accompanied you instead."

That may have indeed been possible if I were in fact the earl's daughter, but since I wasn't, I was subject to Vi's whims. The lowly companion simply would not be allowed to ride without her ladyship. And Vi was indeed terrified of horses.

"I doubt Miss Levine would have cared for riding either," I said.

"She was a stiff-looking woman." He slowed his horse to allow mine to catch up, and we rode side by side. "I'm sorry you had to endure such a grim childhood, Violet. Your life hasn't been fair. I hope...I hope you'll see that it doesn't have to be that way anymore. The thought of being cooped up forever...I don't know how you managed."

"It wasn't so bad. I had a good friend in...Hannah." I swallowed, but the lie stuck in my throat. Perhaps I ought to tell him the truth. Perhaps his uncle really didn't wish Violet ill, and she would be all right at Frakingham, learning to control her talent.

But I needed to be sure. By Christmas I would know for

certain if they meant to harm her. If they proved to be trustworthy, then I would be honest with Jack and help him fetch the real Violet Jamieson.

"I admit that I expected to find you a little mad," he said.

"Oh?"

"I know I would be if I'd been confined to a few rooms my entire life, unable to come or go as I pleased. Yet you're remarkably normal."

I didn't want to venture into a conversation about my life at Windamere. It would be too easy to make a mistake and forget my lie. Particularly because Jack was so perceptive.

"What about you?" I said instead. "What was your childhood like growing up with the ability to start fires?"

He regarded me closely, as if he knew I was deliberately avoiding discussing myself. "It was...fine."

"Your parents weren't alarmed when it first happened?"

"I wouldn't know. I was too young to remember."

"They never talked about it?"

"I mean I was too young to remember them." He urged his horse into a trot, and Clover dutifully followed. The change of pace caught me by surprise, and I bounced uncomfortably along, holding onto the reins for dear life, until we finally came to a stop at the ruins I'd seen on my first day.

All that was left of the abbey were some broken arches, crumbling walls and the lower halves of what must have been sturdy columns at the entrance. Moss had turned many of the stones green, and some structures appeared to only be held together by vines that crawled over everything, claiming the ruins as their own.

"With whom did you live after your parents' deaths?" I asked. Perhaps I should have let the conversation drop, but curiosity was eating at me. I just *had* to know more about Jack Langley. "Sylvia said you didn't come to Frakingham until you were fourteen."

"Don't, Violet." His voice came out choked. "Please." He dismounted and let his horse graze untethered. He patted

Clover's nose and looked up at me from beneath hooded eyes. "A man needs to keep some secrets."

My heart lurched inside my chest, and I suddenly wished to hold him and tell him he could trust me.

But I hardly knew him, and I doubted he'd want a raggedy, freckly redhead throwing herself at him. Besides, I was lying to him, so it seemed only fair that he keep some things from me too.

"I thought it was ladies who were supposed to be the secretive ones," I said.

He looked relieved that the conversation was at an end. "Does this mean that the lovely Lady Violet isn't telling me everything? And here I thought you wore your heart on your sleeve."

"And how do you know what's in my heart, Jack Langley?" I asked softly. I couldn't look away from his eyes, so filled with longing and—dare I even think it let alone hope—desire.

He moved close and skimmed his hand over Clover's neck, toward my knee. He didn't look away, and I certainly couldn't. I was caught in his presence as securely as the ruins in the vines.

His chest rose and fell with his heavy breathing. I waited for him to say something, but he did not. He looked dazed, not quite aware, as he lifted his arms to help me down. He put his hands to my waist, and a shock passed between us, quickly followed by a fierce heat, blasting through me. I felt like I was burning up from the inside.

"Jack!" I screamed.

His eyes widened, but he didn't let me go until my feet were firmly on the ground. Then he stalked off and slapped his hands against his thighs as if he were putting out flames.

I was too busy trying to remove my jacket to check if he'd been burned. I desperately needed to cool down, and the jacket itself smoldered where his hands had been. I was rather glad it was woolen after all.

"Are you all right?" he asked, returning. Worry scored

deep lines into his forehead. He reached for me again, but quickly dropped his hands back to his sides. "Are you hurt?"

"I don't think so. Still a little hot, but I'm beginning to cool. What about you? Your hands must be painful. You weren't wearing gloves, but I at least have some layers to protect me."

"They're fine. Don't worry about me." He crossed his arms and tucked his hands away.

"Let me see." I reached for him.

He stepped back. "Don't touch me!"

I blinked. "Right. Of course."

He strode off and stopped near one of the arches that must have been a doorway once, but now had no walls on either side of it.

I followed. "Jack, let me see your hands."

He blew out a breath then turned around, palms out flat for me to inspect. They were unmarked. No burns, not even a slight reddening.

"They're perfectly fine." I frowned. "But that must have hurt. Your skin was unprotected."

"My skin doesn't burn. Neither does yours. You weren't aware?"

I shook my head.

He fingered the jacket slung over my arm. "It's ruined."

"I'm sorry."

"Whatever for? It's not your fault. It's not mine. It's this cursed *talent*."

"It doesn't feel like a talent, does it?"

"Not always," he muttered.

We stood in silence until I could stand it no longer. I was bursting with questions. "You said you don't burn."

"*We* don't burn. Not our skin anyway."

"That doesn't make sense. Are you saying there's some part of you that does burn?"

He pressed his lips together and for a moment I thought he'd refuse to answer. "You ought to know," he said. "Since it affects you too."

"Jack, you're scaring me."

He went to reach for me again, but stopped himself and let his hand fall. "Have you heard of spontaneous combustion?"

"That's when someone burns, yet there's no evidence of how they caught alight, isn't it? I always thought it was a hoax or a way of covering up a murder."

"Perhaps it is. Perhaps not."

"Oh God." I felt the color drain from my face, and the lingering heat too. "Are you saying that you—we—can spontaneously combust?"

"I don't know for sure since you and I are the only fire starters in existence and neither of us has suffered that fate, obviously. But when the sparks come I feel like I'm boiling inside. Ever since I heard of spontaneous combustion I've wondered if that's how those people died. If they were like me, burning up inside."

"Oh," I whispered. "But you can control your fire, can't you?"

He lifted his gaze to mine. "The sparks and heat come only when I'm very angry. Or so I thought."

"You're not angry now."

He turned away. "No."

"Then...why? I don't understand."

"It's not important."

"It *is* important!"

"Don't, Violet." He spun back round, and I was shocked by how pink his cheeks were. From the fire within him?

I reeled back. "I'm sorry. Don't be angry with me."

The color quickly vanished and his face turned ashen. "Violet, I'm not angry with you. I doubt I ever could be." Again he went to reach for me, and again he lowered his arms before we touched. "Bloody hell," he muttered. "I hate this."

I sat on the base of what must have once been a column. I watched him as he too sat on a large stone and picked at the long grass licking up its sides. He seemed to be avoiding my gaze on purpose.

"I've seen you hold Sylvia's hand before and that didn't happen," I said. "You patted Clover's nose and nothing. Indeed, when you kidnapped me, you touched me. Admittedly I passed out, but I'm sure I would have felt that heat beforehand if it had been there. So why now, Jack? What was different about this time?"

"Do you have to ask?" he muttered.

"Yes, and you must answer. If you're going to let off sparks every time we touch now, I need to know."

He scrubbed a hand across his chin and lower lip, all the while avoiding my gaze. "August warned me before I went to spy on you that if we developed feelings for one another, we may not be able to control the fire when we...uh...that is, at certain moments."

Oh. Oh! He had feelings for me? Me? The little freckly redhead from the attic? I tried to think of something to say, but I knew I'd sound like a blathering fool, so I bit my tongue and concentrated on remaining unruffled. Unfortunately he wasn't looking at me and my efforts went unnoticed.

He grunted a harsh, humorless laugh. "I don't know what bothers me more. That you know I have feelings for you, or that August was right. It didn't matter when he first told me." A beat passed before he added, "It does now."

I pressed my hand to my chest. My heart felt like it was being squeezed by a fist. "Do you mean that your feelings for me have grown so that now when we touch, we may combust?"

He jerked a thumb at Clover, nibbling the grass contentedly beside her stable mate. "I only held you at your waist. Imagine if we...kissed."

I touched my lips. "Yes. Imagine."

His mouth gave a harsh twist. "Ironic that I finally find a girl I like, but a single kiss could kill her."

"And you," I whispered. "It could kill you too."

CHAPTER 7

The mist rolled in while Jack and I sat in silence. It draped the ruins like a ghostly veil, and only the taller structures rose above it. The cooler, damper air doused the last remnants of heat inside me. It could not, however, dampen my raging thoughts. There were so many, and picking them apart proved impossible.

"We'd better go back," Jack said, standing. "I'd offer my hand to assist you, but I don't think that's wise."

I rose unassisted and put on my jacket. I would have to mount Clover without aid too.

Jack must have been thinking the same thing because he led my horse to the column base I'd been sitting on. "Stand up there and put your left foot in the stirrup." He held the stirrup for me and I did as suggested, careful not to touch him.

Once I was safely in the saddle, he mounted too. His horse shifted restlessly, as if he wanted to race off, but Jack soothed him with gentle words.

Clover moved behind the other horse, and my gaze shifted to Jack's broad back and shoulders. They were strong, capable shoulders and looked magnificent straining the seams of his riding jacket.

Now that the shock of discovering that he liked me had worn off, I was able to think about our situation more clearly. Or rather, *my* situation. I should have told him that he had the wrong girl. I should have told him about the real Violet Jamieson. She needed the training, not me. She needed to know there was someone else like her.

The lie was beginning to eat me up inside, turning me cold where the heat of Jack's blast had warmed me only moments ago. Would he ignite like that if he touched Vi? Or had that only happened because he liked *me*, and it was something only *I* had the power to do?

Despite my doubts, the notion that Langley would use Vi as a test case still gnawed at me. If it were just August Langley who'd kidnapped me, I would have been certain that he wanted Vi so he could study her, but it was Jack and Sylvia's involvement that threw water over that theory. They *seemed* quite harmless. What I needed was a test of my own to determine once and for all if I could trust Jack.

"Are the police following up that information you gave them about the boot print?"

He half turned in the saddle to look back at me. "Why do you ask?"

"I'm simply curious. Don't you think it's unusual that a thief entered the house, stole some papers, then got out again without anyone seeing him?"

He focused on the path ahead once more, but I saw the slight stiffening of his back. "Unusual, but not impossible. It's a big house."

"Yes, but not one single servant heard or saw him."

"What are you getting at, Violet?"

"Just that I'm surprised none of them mentioned seeing or hearing an intruder to you." He made no comment, so I asked as boldly as I could. "They didn't, did they?"

"No."

My heart sank. It was an outright lie. He'd told Tommy that the maid named Maud had described the intruder to him. I swallowed the bitter taste in my mouth.

"When we go to London, will you be staying with Sylvia and me the entire time?"

His hesitation was small, but it was there. "If you wish me to."

I urged Clover to speed up and she trotted alongside Jack's horse. He glanced at me then away. "You won't be going to visit people you used to know there?" I asked.

"I don't know what you're talking about."

"Your accent sounds cultured now, but when you grew angry in your uncle's rooms, it changed."

"A person's manner of speaking can do that when they're ruled by their emotions."

"Yes, but they don't switch to London slum accents. I wondered if you would visit your old friends upon your return, and if you'll take Sylvia and me with you."

He turned to me again. His jaw was set as hard as stone, his eyes even harder. "How do you know what a London slum accent sounds like, Violet? Heard many while locked away in the attic of a grand house?" He squeezed his horse's flanks and the big animal set off at a gallop.

By the time Clover reached the stables, my rear was sore and my heart sorer. Jack was nowhere to be seen.

**

"You got back all right?" Jack asked me the next day as we waited in the entrance hall for the carriage to be brought around.

"No thanks to you." I'd spent half the night wondering if I'd lost a potential friend and the other half considering what I ought to do. By the time I finally fell asleep, I'd decided I needed more time before I admitted that I was not Violet Jamieson. Jack was keeping too many secrets, and until I found out if they would endanger Vi, I would pretend to be her. I was utterly convinced that August Langley's reasons for kidnapping me weren't purely charitable, and I suspected Jack's lies were somehow tied in with his uncle's. All I needed to do was unravel them so that I could make a clear decision.

"It was unforgiveable of me to leave you like that," he said. "And for speaking harshly. I'm sorry."

I had still not come to terms with the fact he'd lied to me, and after he said he liked me too! Jack Langley was more of a mystery than ever. I wasn't about to make life easy for him. "It was unforgiveable."

He sucked in a breath. "I suppose I deserved that. I'll have you know that I didn't neglect you altogether. I checked not half an hour later, and Olson said you made it back in one piece shortly after me."

"I could have been lying dead in a ditch by then, and no one would have known."

Tommy approached and handed Jack his coat and gloves. Jack slung the coat over his arm and clutched the gloves. "Olson would have alerted me immediately if Clover had turned up riderless."

"That may have cost valuable time."

"If you'd been dead, there wouldn't have been any hurry, would there?"

I gave him a withering look, and he gave me a triumphant smile. Tommy smirked in the background, but sobered when I switched my glare to him.

"I notice you've been avoiding me ever since," I said to Jack. "Any reason for that?"

"None in particular."

The carriage pulled up in front of the house, laden with our luggage. Sylvia descended the stairs wrapped in fur from head to toe. "Are you two arguing?" she said. "It's going to be a long journey if you are."

Jack walked outside, ignoring her.

"Everything's fine." I caught up to Jack. "You can't avoid me now," I said. "You'll have to endure my company all the way to London."

He held the door open and Tommy helped me inside, then he did the same for Sylvia. She sat opposite me as Jack shut the door without getting in. I pushed the window down and poked my head out. He doffed his hat, gave me another one of those irritatingly smug smiles, then sprang up onto the driver's seat alongside Olson.

I sat back heavily and clicked my tongue. "Your cousin is..." I couldn't think of what to call him. The truth was, I liked Jack and he liked me. I just wished he hadn't lied to me.

"Infuriating?" Sylvia offered. "Stubborn? Secretive? Volatile?"

"Secretive, yes! Tell me about his past. He said his parents died when he was young, yet he didn't come to live here with your uncle until he was fourteen. What did he do in between? Where did he live?"

She stroked the fur collar of her coat near her chin to flatten it. "It's not my place to tell you. Besides, I'm not really sure of the entire story myself. Be patient. He'll tell you in time."

Time. How much did I have?

***

London was nothing like I expected. I thought it would be all gleaming glass windows and vibrant color, but the reality was quite different. It was gray. Gray buildings, gray muddy roads and gray air. Even the people were dressed in gray, their faces merely a paler shade of the same color. The smells of horse dung and factory fumes clung to the city, and I insisted Sylvia keep the carriage window closed.

"It's been so long since we've been here," she murmured, her nose pressed to the pane. "I'd quite forgotten what it was like. Look, there's a milliner's, and another, and...my goodness, there's four on this street alone!"

"You'll be sure to find a hat you like then."

"And you too."

"You forget I haven't any money. There was no opportunity to ask Lord Wade for an allowance before I came."

"Don't be like that, Violet. Uncle will buy you anything you want."

"I doubt his generosity will extend to extra hats considering he's already provided several, thanks to you."

She turned her bright smile on me. "Don't be silly! Of course he will. Anyway, Jack's in control of the money and he won't deny you anything."

I smoothed down my skirts, intent on ignoring the rush of blood to my face that betrayed my thoughts. "Hasn't your uncle given you an allowance of your own to spend any way you like? Why must you rely on Jack?"

"Because that's the way Uncle wishes it. Who am I to gainsay him?"

"Perhaps you ought to try," I said, but she mustn't have heard me. She was too busy bouncing up and down, pointing at a confectioner's shop.

"We'll be sure to visit there," she said. "I long for something sweet, a tart perhaps. Oh, and bonbons since Christmas isn't far away. I wonder how long before we arrive at our hotel."

She chatted on as the carriage drove down streets bustling with late afternoon shoppers, pointing out things that took her fancy, which was almost everything. Her enthusiasm was infectious, however, and I too became engrossed in the sights through the window. London was truly an amazing city, and extensive. We seemed to be driving through it forever.

But what really took my breath away was the lack of nature. No trees, no grass, not even a bird flew overhead. Not that I would have seen it anyway through the murky haze. Indeed, the only thing flapping up high were washed linens hung out to dry in some of the narrow alleys we passed. How anything dried in that filthy, damp air was a mystery.

The carriage turned a few more corners, winding its way through the traffic, until finally the buildings became more magnificent and the pedestrians fewer and better clothed. This part of London at least seemed a little less gray than the rest.

"We're here," Sylvia said as the carriage slowed. "Claridges."

We pulled up at an impressive red brick building, and a liveried footman opened the carriage door for us. Jack jumped down from the driver's seat as the footman helped me down the carriage steps. More servants retrieved our luggage and carried it inside.

"Did you know that royalty has stayed here?" Sylvia said to me as we crossed the tiled floor of the entrance hall.

"It's very grand." The ceiling was high and the room enormous, much like Windamere's entrance hall. Indeed, the opulent furnishings and gleaming surfaces made it seem very similar to Lord Wade's home. I dared not touch anything lest one of the hovering footmen frown at me. At least at Frakingham the furniture was more functional and the servants scarce. For the first time since my abduction, I wished I was there.

***

"I can assure you Lady Violet will be quite safe," said the little man with ruddy cheeks and several chins. He sat on one side of a very broad desk, his younger assistant beside him. Jack, Sylvia and I sat opposite. "Mr. Gladstone is very good at inducing a state of hypnosis in—"

"Your assistant!" Jack shook his head. "No. I want *you* to do it, Dr. Werner. Someone with experience."

Dr. Werner's glasses slid down his nose but were rescued by the upturned tip. He pushed them back up and gave Jack what could only be described as a practiced professional smile. "I can assure you, Mr. Langley, Mr. Gladstone is very good. He may be only a young man, but being a youthful gentleman yourself, you'll know that age is not necessarily a good indicator of a person's abilities. Mr. Gladstone has never failed to put my patients into a hypnotic state. Never."

Jack narrowed his eyes at the assistant, a handsome sandy-haired man with clear blue eyes and a mischievous mouth that hadn't stopped smiling since we entered Dr. Werner's medical rooms. Mr. Gladstone's happy countenance was in stark contrast to Jack's dark mood. He hadn't stopped peppering poor Dr. Werner with questions since our arrival.

"Is he a qualified hypnotist?" Jack asked.

"I'm studying medicine at University College here in London," Mr. Gladstone said, speaking for the first time. "I'll graduate next year."

"We're neurologists," Dr. Werner added. "Hypnotist is not a medical occupation."

"*You* are a neurologist," Jack said. "*He* is not yet qualified."

Dr. Werner sighed. "Mr. Langley, will you allow your friend to undergo treatment or not?"

"It's a little late to have doubts now, Jack," Sylvia said, checking the small pocket watch she kept in her reticule.

"It won't hurt," Mr. Gladstone said to me. "There won't be any ill effects after you come out of hypnosis." His smile was so warm and genuine that I couldn't *not* believe him.

"It's what will happen *during* hypnosis that concerns me," Jack said.

"Then you're welcome to stay and watch as long as you keep out of the way."

"I intend to."

"It's settled then," said Sylvia. "Begin, Mr. Gladstone."

I suddenly felt like I wanted to run out of the room. I knew nothing about hypnosis. Did it hurt? And what if they discovered the truth while I was in a hypnotic state? What if I said something I shouldn't, something that would lead them to the truth of who I was?

"You may wait for me outside," I told Jack and Sylvia.

Jack blinked then leaned closer. "Violet, I don't think you should be alone with these men. We don't know much about them."

"Dr. Werner came highly recommended by your uncle," I whispered back. At his troubled look, I added, "You don't trust your uncle?"

"I don't make a habit of it." He squeezed the bridge of his nose and closed his eyes. He looked like he carried the weight of the world, and I desperately wanted to touch him in some way, tell him that he needn't feel burdened. But I dared not. Could not.

"Jack, please. I'll be all right."

"I give you my word that she will be unharmed," Mr. Gladstone said, coming out from behind the desk.

"As do I," said Dr. Werner, rather irritably. "Indeed, I can ill afford to upset my patients now, can I?"

Jack gave a single nod, albeit a reluctant one.

Mr. Gladstone held out his hand for me and I took it. Jack glowered and stalked off toward the door. "Are you sure, Violet?"

"Yes."

Sylvia took his arm and steered him out then shut the door.

"Lie down on the sofa," said Dr. Werner. I did, with Mr. Gladstone's assistance. "Now, it would help if you told us what is being blocked."

I glanced at the door. "Memories."

"Of what?"

"Of..."

"Go on, Lady Violet," said Mr. Gladstone in a soothing voice. "Whatever you tell us will remain in confidence if you wish, as will our findings from the hypnosis itself. If you don't want anyone else to know, then we'll not divulge a thing."

Dr. Werner patted my hand. "Tell us what you know of the memories that are blocked, Lady Violet. Indeed, what makes you think you have some missing memories at all?"

"I fall asleep with no warning," I said. "At least, I believe there's no warning. That's the part I can't remember. Whatever happens just before I fall asleep is lost to me."

"You're a narcoleptic?" Dr. Werner said. "Interesting."

"Not from my point of view."

"From a medical perspective it is. You're unique. Memory loss is not normally a symptom of narcolepsy."

"Then it would seem I'm not normal."

Mr. Gladstone smiled. "Let's see what we can discover

during the hypnosis." He picked up a gold disc attached to a chain. "Concentrate on this object and my voice, Lady Violet." How could I not? The disc was right above my nose and his voice slid against my skin and melted through to my bones. I felt like I was sinking into it, surrounded by it, lost in it. "Your body is feeling heavy. Your eyes want to close. Close them, Lady Violet. Listen to my voice."

I heard nothing more as I slipped away.

***

"Well?" I said, sitting up on the sofa. "What did you learn?"

The two hypnotists stood beside me just as they had done before I fell asleep. Both frowned.

"Nothing," Dr. Werner said, adjusting his glasses. "Absolutely nothing, I'm afraid. There is indeed something blocking access to that compartment."

"Compartment?"

Mr. Gladstone sat on a chair nearby. He didn't look at me, but down at his palms.

Dr. Werner retrieved a clay model of a head that had been sitting on a table near the window. It was cut in half to reveal the brain inside. "Everything about us—our memories, our abilities and thoughts—are stored in different areas of our brains." He pointed to various parts of the head. "On rare occasions, access to these are blocked off. The blockage is usually caused by an accident, but I've known of cases where some other sort of traumatic experience has closed off the compartment where the memory of the experience is contained. It's the brain's way of coping with the event. Usually hypnosis will reveal to us what that event was, and by discussing it with the patient afterward, we're able to permanently unblock the blockage."

"But not with me?"

Mr. Gladstone looked up and shook his head. "Not with you, Lady Violet."

"What does that mean?"

The two men exchanged concerned glances. "It's almost

impossible to say," Mr. Gladstone said.

Dr. Werner cleared his throat. "In all likelihood, it means the event was so traumatic that your mind wouldn't cope if the compartment were unblocked, and the memories became accessible again."

Mr. Gladstone winced as if he'd not wanted his employer to reveal that much. He opened his mouth to say something then shut it again and returned to studying his hands.

"I see," I said. "Well, thank you for your help." I stood and hardly noticed when Mr. Gladstone stood too and took my elbow. I felt distant, removed, as if we'd just been discussing another patient and not my own situation. Perhaps the hypnosis hadn't quite worn off completely.

"I'll call in your friends," Dr. Werner said.

"Wait. Before you do, tell me, what would it take to unblock that compartment?"

He paused at the door and glanced once more at Mr. Gladstone beside me. I felt the assistant stiffen and heard the air hiss between his teeth. "I don't know, Lady Violet. You may never regain those memories. That may not be a bad thing, however."

Jack was standing just outside the door when Mr. Gladstone opened it. "Were you listening in?" I asked him.

"No!" he said, unblinking. "Not at all."

Sylvia made a miffed sound through her nose. "The door was too thick to hear anything through it."

"I wanted to make sure you came to no harm," Jack said.

"I'm quite all right. Thank you, Dr. Werner, Mr. Gladstone."

"Wait a moment." Jack held up a hand. "What happened? What did you learn?"

"Nothing, I'm afraid," Dr. Werner said. "I'm sorry your visit to London has been a waste of time."

"Not a waste at all, Doctor," said Sylvia. "We have other activities to pursue during our stay."

He bowed to her then to me. "I bid you good day, ladies. Mr. Langley."

Mr. Gladstone took my hand and held it in a grip that had me quite alarmed with its firmness. "It was a pleasure to meet you, Lady Violet. Perhaps...perhaps you'll come again and we'll have more success next time."

"Or not," said Jack. "Send the account to Claridges. We leave in the morning."

We left, but the feeling that Mr. Gladstone was unsettled never left me. Whatever the reason, he mustn't have shared it with the doctor. I should have questioned him, but a very big part of me didn't want to know. I had the horrible feeling it was related to the trauma Dr. Werner mentioned. I didn't want to dwell upon that at all. For now, I was of the opinion that what I didn't know couldn't harm me.

Perhaps if I kept telling myself that, I might even have believed it.

"Are you all right?" Sylvia asked when we were in the carriage.

Jack lounged back on the seat and rubbed his hands down his face, over his jaw.

"Go ahead," I said. "I know it's killing you not to ask."

He huffed out a breath. "Did they...did anything...? Oh bloody hell. I should have stayed with you in there."

"Calm down. Nothing untoward happened. You heard Dr. Werner say that his reputation is of the utmost importance to him."

"So what did they do?" Sylvia asked. "What did it feel like?"

I shrugged. "Like I couldn't keep my eyes open. Mr. Gladstone's voice was simply..." I shook my head, unable to describe its rich, modular tones, the way it hummed through my mind.

"I know," Sylvia muttered. "His voice was as handsome as his face."

"I'm not quite sure that's how I'd explain it."

"So you just fell asleep?" Jack asked. "Then what?"

"Then I woke up. How long was I in the room?"

"Only ten minutes," he said. "You didn't experience

anything while you were in a hypnotic state?"

"Not a thing. No dreams, no consciousness of what was happening in the real world. Nothing."

"Remarkable," Sylvia said, shaking her head in wonder. "What skill that Mr. Gladstone has. And to think, he's only an apprentice."

"August will be disappointed it came to nothing," Jack said.

"It was your idea," Sylvia pointed out.

"Doesn't mean it was a good one." He turned to look out the window and she winked at me. She did enjoy vexing her cousin, but he didn't seem in the mood to toss it back as he usually did.

**

Fortunately my mind was kept from wandering back to Dr. Werner's rooms and the hypnosis by an afternoon of shopping. An *entire* afternoon. By four o'clock, Jack declared he'd had enough and insisted we return to the hotel. "You've been into every milliner, dressmaker and perfumer on Oxford Street and beyond, some of them twice," he said. "There's only so much a man can stand. Besides, Violet's feet are sore."

"Don't stop on my account," I said.

"You're limping."

So he'd noticed that. My feet ached like the devil, and if I had to suffer through one more shop assistant uttering false sympathies about my hair color or bust size, I'd scream. I knew pink didn't suit me, but did they need to hold a swathe of silk in that color up to my face at every turn then *tsk tsk* over the effect? It was as if they delighted in revealing how unfashionable I was. Perhaps that was the whole point. An uncommon number of them seemed to be trying to catch Jack's attention, and once they learned I was a friend and not a relation like Sylvia, the claws came out. It made me long for the attic and solitude. Well, perhaps it wasn't quite that bad, but I'd stopped enjoying myself hours earlier.

"Just one more shop," said Sylvia. "I'm yet to find a hat in just the right shade of gray."

Jack looked heavenward and sighed.

"You could wait in the carriage," I said. Olson had followed us along Oxford Street, our purchases in the storage compartment at the back of the carriage. We had, however, decided to walk so that Sylvia could have a closer look through the windows and see which shops she wanted to enter. It turned out that she wanted to enter every single one.

"I'll come with you," Jack said. "Here's a milliner's you haven't been to yet. Let's get it over with."

He held the door open and we entered. Several heads swiveled toward us, some belonging to the shop assistants, and others to the shoppers. It seemed we were quite the objects of curiosity wherever we went, and this time was no exception. Their gazes quickly took in both Sylvia and I before settling upon Jack. Then the flirting began. Some simply stared at him, but the more outgoing girls sidled close, pretending to be interested in something nearby. One or two even spoke to him outright, which I thought incredibly forward since they hadn't been introduced.

"Jack does appear to be popular here in London," I said to Sylvia as we inspected the hats on display.

"Of course," she said with a laugh. "He's young, single, handsome and clearly a gentleman of means. Most of these women have been watching us all afternoon, some even following us."

I watched Jack standing by the door, trying not to make eye contact with anyone, including me. If he knew he was being ogled, he didn't show it. His ignorance didn't last long, however. A woman shopping with her daughter approached, smiling like a clown at a circus.

"Excuse me, but you're Mr. Bellamy, aren't you?" she said to Jack.

He bowed. "No, madam. My name is Langley."

The woman's smile didn't waver. "Indeed? I do apologize. You resemble my friend Bellamy to a certain degree."

"I'm sure he doesn't," Sylvia muttered.

"You think she lied?" I whispered back.

"If Bellamy were indeed her friend, she'd know what he looked like."

"Then why the ruse?"

"She has a daughter of marriageable age." She nodded at the girl of seventeen or so who observed her mother out of the corner of her eye. "They probably think Jack is a potential suitor, and the mother wants to be the first of her acquaintance to engage his interest. Keep listening."

A shop girl approached and Sylvia left me to be shown some hats at the back. I continued to watch Jack from beneath lowered lashes as I strolled between tables and hat stands.

"You must be new to London, Mr. Langley," the woman said. "I've never seen you at any of the parties."

"I come to the city rarely, and only for business. I live in Hertfordshire, madam, with my uncle, August Langley."

A small crease connected her thin eyebrows. "That name sounds familiar. Where in Hertfordshire is your uncle's house, Mr. Langley? Perhaps that will refresh my memory."

"Frakingham House, near Harborough."

The woman's mouth pursed as if she'd tasted something bitter. "Oh." She stepped away. "Good day to you, sir. My apologies for mistaking you for my friend. I can see now that you're nothing like Mr. Bellamy." She scuttled away and rejoined her daughter.

"Mama?" the girl whispered. "What's wrong?"

The mother's voice was too low for me to hear her entire answer. The only words I could make out were "Freak House." It was enough to explain her change in behavior.

Sylvia bought two hats in different shades of gray, and Jack carried the boxes out to the carriage and bundled them into the storage compartment with the others. "Satisfied now, Cousin?" he asked Sylvia as he settled opposite us on the seat.

"Why are those women looking at us like we have two heads?" she said.

I followed her gaze to the woman who'd questioned Jack and her daughter. They did indeed eye us from beneath their hat brims. "You were right about them," I told her. "The mother wished to throw her daughter into Jack's path at any parties he might deign to attend."

Jack rolled his eyes.

"Yes, but why does she look as if she wants to run in the other direction to get away from us?" She narrowed her eyes at him. "What did you say to her?"

"Nothing," he said. "I gave her my name and place of residence, that's all."

Sylvia flounced back into the seat and crossed her arms. "How *could* you?" One corner of his mouth lifted and her glare sharpened. "It's not amusing."

"I'm sorry," he said, sobering. "I know it matters to you. I just wish you knew that they don't matter to me."

"What doesn't?" I said. "I don't understand."

"Whenever we go anywhere, which isn't often, Jack likes to tell people where we're from."

"It's called introducing myself, Syl. It's what people do when they meet."

"Yes, but can't you lie? Why do you have to tell them we're from Frakingham?"

"Because we are. The sooner you come to accept that, the happier you'll be."

"I doubt I could ever be happy to be associated with Freak House."

Jack looked quite unnerved by her misery. "Those people aren't for the likes of us," he said quietly.

"You shouldn't let them bother you," I said to her. "I agree with Jack. They don't seem like the sort of people you'd want to be friends with anyway."

"That's easy for you to say. You and Jack *are* the freaks. I'm the freak by association. It's not fair."

Her remark cut through me to the bone. I'd thought we'd

become friends of sorts, but to say something so offhandedly callous proved there was still an ocean of differences between us. She was right, of course. I wasn't normal. Now I knew I was also very much alone.

We arrived at Claridges, and instead of coming inside with us, Jack bid us farewell. "I'm going for a walk," he said.

"Where to?" Sylvia asked.

"Nowhere in particular. I need to stretch my legs."

"You've been walking all day."

"You object to me wanting to spend some time alone?"

"Do whatever you want," she said huffily, striding off.

I watched Jack go and chewed my lip. Should I follow him? If I did, would I learn more about him? I knew he was going to see Patrick, the person he suspected of breaking into Frakingham House, and I desperately wanted to find out who Patrick was and how Jack knew him. But I would have to follow him surreptitiously, and that meant being alone, more or less. I didn't consider myself a fearful person in general, but being on my own in a city the size of London set my nerves on edge. What if I lost Jack? What if I wandered into one of the less appealing areas I'd seen on our journey in?

"Lady Violet!" called a familiar voice.

"Mr. Gladstone!" I said as he came up to me. "Are you here to see me?"

"I am. May we talk?"

Down the street, Jack turned the corner, unaware of the medical student's presence. I made up my mind then and there. "Yes! Excellent. Let's talk and walk at the same time. I have a mind to be out and about in this fresh air."

He pulled a face. "It's cold and growing dark."

"The lamps will be lit soon. I've always wanted to see London in the evening." I hooked my arm through his and hailed one of the Claridges' footmen hovering nearby. "Please inform Miss Langley that I've gone for a walk," I told him. To Mr. Gladstone I said, "Quickly now. A swift walk is a good one." We rounded a corner, and I breathed a sigh of relief when I saw Jack up ahead. "Now, what is it you wanted to say to me, Mr. Gladstone?"

CHAPTER 8

"Lady Violet, is everything all right?" Mr. Gladstone asked. "You seem distracted."

"Just enjoying the walk. And please, let's not be so formal with one another. You may call me Violet." *Hannah*, part of me shouted inside. I so wished to hear my real name again.

"In that case, you may call me Samuel."

Up ahead, Jack turned another corner. He walked swiftly, his strides long and purposeful. He didn't look back, and since it was becoming darker, we didn't need to hide. London's ever-present fog had already begun to settle in the dim depths of the alleys, and it wasn't yet four o'clock.

"Now, Samuel, what is it you wanted to talk to me about?"

"May we slow down?"

"No."

"Right." He cleared this throat. "Ever since you left Dr. Werner's rooms this morning, I haven't been able to stop thinking about you. I mean, your situation."

"Oh?" Jack turned another corner and I sped up. I didn't want to lose him when we'd gotten this far.

"I think there may be another possibility to explain the blocking of your memories."

"Something other than a traumatic event? That is a relief." Indeed it was. I'd felt unnerved at the thought ever since he'd suggested it.

"Yes, but..." He sighed. "There's no easy way to tell you this. Someone may have deliberately tampered with your mind."

I stumbled, but with our arms linked, he was able to steady me. I stared up at him, my heart in my throat, beating like a drum. "You'd better tell me what you mean."

"We'll lose him if we don't keep walking," he said.

"Pardon?"

He nodded in the direction of Jack. "Mr. Langley. We are following him, aren't we?"

I pressed a hand to my head. "Yes," I murmured. "But this is...important."

"Then I'll tell you as we go. Come on."

I allowed him to lead me a few paces until I regained my wits. "Samuel, tell me, please. What do you mean someone has tampered with my mind? Do you mean they've blocked off my memories on purpose?"

"*May* have blocked them. It's simply another possibility. One I didn't want to mention in front of Dr. Werner."

"Why not?"

"Because he doesn't believe in it."

"Believe in what? Samuel, you're not making sense."

He huffed out a breath. "This is complicated, but I'll try to explain it. I've been able to hypnotize people ever since I can remember. Medical professionals like Dr. Werner have had to learn to do it, but I've always had the ability."

"Really? Have you been hypnotizing unsuspecting people since you were a child?"

He gave me a crooked smile. "Yes, much to my parents' dismay, until..." He cleared his throat. "Never mind. Suffice it to say, I learned not to use hypnosis unless the subject agreed. I decided the best way to use my ability was to become a neurologist and hypnotize patients in a professional capacity."

"When did you discover that memories could be blocked? Is that something you can do?"

"Do you always ask so many questions?"

"Yes. The Langleys find it irritating too."

He chuckled. "Come on, walk faster. He's going into that alley."

Jack had indeed entered a narrow street through an archway. We paused at its entrance, then when we saw him walking up ahead, we continued on. The houses changed. They were smaller and squashed together like cold, ragged children. Their windows and stoops, however, were clean and those people still outside appeared to have somewhere to go, although there was hollow resignation on their faces.

I drew closer to Samuel. "Are you all right, Violet? Do you want to turn back?"

"No. I expected we would be entering one of the worst areas of London."

"This isn't the worst," he said quietly. "Not by far." If he were afraid, he didn't show it. He did seem particularly alert, scanning to left and right as we walked.

"Go on, Samuel. Tell me about purposefully blocking memories using hypnosis."

"I stumbled upon the process in my teens. I was, uh, experimenting with my abilities, and unfortunately instead of hypnotizing someone and making him think he was a woman, I blocked his memory of the entire day."

"You tried to make a man think he was a woman?" I giggled. "You can do that?"

"There are many things a hypnotist can do while a subject is in a hypnotized state. That was one of my favorites when I was about fifteen."

"How wicked of you."

"I can assure you, my wickedness is in the past. These days I mostly cure ladies of melancholy or hysteria," he said with a sigh. "You are a welcome change."

The street narrowed again and the air grew dank, dark. Very little light filtered through the fog from the setting sun.

There were few gas lamps, and even fewer of them were lit. Those that were lit glowed in the miasma like disembodied orbs.

"So what happened after you tried to hypnotize that man into thinking he was a woman?"

"When the subject awoke from his hypnosis, something very odd happened. He became a narcoleptic."

"What!"

"Shhh."

Up ahead, Jack stopped. Samuel pulled me into a recessed doorway as Jack turned. My face pressed into Samuel's chest. I could feel his chin above my head, his heart thumping against my ear despite the layers of clothing. It beat in time to the rhythm of my blood.

He peered round the edge of the brickwork. "He's walking again."

We followed. "Did your subject fall asleep at particular moments, or did the narcoleptic episodes occur with no pattern whatsoever?"

"He fell asleep at...moments of great...excitement."

"How interesting. Does he still suffer from the episodes?"

"No."

"Did you cure him?"

"I tried but couldn't. He was cured in another way."

"How?"

A few heartbeats passed before he answered. "It's not something I can discuss with a lady."

"Samuel, you have to tell me. Whatever it is, I can assure you I won't be shocked."

He cleared his throat. "Very well. Yes, it took another event of great excitement to cure him. Excitement of a...male nature."

"You mean when he was aroused by a woman?"

He made a strangled sound that I took as embarrassed affirmation.

"I do believe you're blushing, Samuel." As was I, rather

fiercely. Despite my attempt to sound worldly, I was very far from it. I knew in theory what happened between a man and a woman when they grew aroused, thanks to a book our biology tutor smuggled in one day while Miss Levine wasn't looking, but my practical knowledge was nil.

"Well," he said. "So. In conclusion, whatever produces narcolepsy within *you*, is the very thing that will cure you of it, albeit in a larger dose. My subject fell asleep when he was aroused, but it was the same emotion that ended his narcolepsy once and for all."

"A larger dose?"

"My subject was cured by excessive, ah, stimulation. There happened to be two women with him at the time."

"Two! Is that even possible?"

Poor Samuel ran his finger inside his collar and stretched his neck. "Please don't ask any more questions. There are some things a lady shouldn't hear."

What about a lady's companion?

"You need to expose yourself to whatever emotion it is that sets off your narcolepsy," he said. "Do you know what it is?"

"Fear, I think."

"Good. All you need now is to experience heightened terror, and you may be cured."

"That's something to look forward to," I said dryly.

"Who do you think did this to you? You must know someone capable of hypnosis. Someone with the natural talent for it like me, not learned as in Dr. Werner's case. Do you know who that might be?"

"No. Nor do I know why they would do this to me."

"Tell me about the Langleys. Perhaps it was one of them."

"It wasn't. I've only known them a few days, and I've been a narcoleptic all my life."

"Indeed? What about your family?"

"I'm not in contact with them at the moment. When I see them again I'll ask."

"A good idea."

"You say Dr. Werner doesn't believe in this kind of blockage, as put there by a hypnotist. That means you must have discussed it with him at some point."

"I have, but he tried to replicate it and it didn't work. When I suggested that only natural hypnotists could do it, he scoffed and said there were no such people."

"How odd."

"Very. I don't know of others, you see, and have heard of none. You don't know what it's like to be the only one who suffers from something."

How wrong he was.

"You're the first person I've mentioned my ability to," he said. "I have to say, it's such a relief that you're not laughing at me, or have run screaming in the other direction."

"I wouldn't do that. I may need you if I fall asleep out here."

We hurried after Jack, getting further and further into the depths of London's web of alleys. "I'm beginning to think we ought to turn back," Samuel said. "This part of London isn't safe, particularly after dark."

We had indeed walked into an even grimier part of the city. The cobbled streets were covered in some sort of slippery sludge. I had to hold onto Samuel's arm or I'd slip over. A sickly smell mingled with the fog that hung in the air. Dirty children's faces peered out of windows at us, their eyes sunken, their hair matted. Men and women sat or lay on the filthy ground, their hands buried in their too-thin clothes, their feet and heads bare, despite winter being in the air. One or two clutched my hem as I passed, begging for food, and Samuel quickly obliged with a few coins until he had no more to give.

I clung to his arm and slowed. "You're right. We should go back."

Just as I said it, Jack stopped to talk to a boy shivering in a recessed doorway. He nodded, and the lad disappeared inside, only to return a moment later with a tall man. A man with a big, crooked nose and a scar over one eye. He clamped Jack on the shoulder and Jack nodded a greeting. The thin lad scampered back inside and shut the door.

I looked around for closer hiding places and spotted an arched bridge nearby. If we stood beneath it, we would be able to hear their conversation. "Keep your head down and stay close to the walls where it's darker," I said to Samuel.

"What if he sees us?"

"He won't harm us, if that's your concern. I am quite sure of that."

"He won't harm *you*. I doubt any feelings of mercy will extend to me."

"Are you afraid of him?"

"No, I just don't want to have to fight him. I put those days behind me when I started at University College."

"You were a fighter?"

"I got into scrapes regularly and found the need to defend myself." He put a hand to his hat to shield his face. It didn't matter because Jack was too intent on his conversation to notice us. We tucked ourselves into the shadows of the archway and strained to hear.

"I confess," said Jack's companion. "It were me that done it. You goin' to drag me off to the rozzers then?" He sounded amused, cock-sure.

"I should. Or better yet, I'll take you home with me. August Langley will have a fitting punishment in mind."

"Stop speakin' like a toff." The man, Patrick I assumed, wiped his nose with the back of his hand. "You ain't one of 'em. Never will be. Think you're all 'igh and mighty livin' in the big 'ouse while we starve down 'ere in this rat-pit." He hawked and spat on the ground at Jack's feet.

Jack didn't move, but his shoulders stiffened slightly, and his hands closed into fists at his sides. "What did you take from his rooms?"

"I dunno, do I. Just some papers. I was told where to find 'em and find 'em I did."

"Papers about what?"

"That some kind of joke? You know I can't read."

Jack tipped his head back, sighed. "Who are you working for?"

"I can't tell you that now, Jack-o'-Lantern. Ain't none o' your business no more."

"It is my business. I live there."

Patrick snorted a harsh laugh. "And what right 'ave *you* got to live there? Eh? You fink that man's yer uncle? Because I ain't so sure you're any more a Langley than me."

Jack shoved Patrick in the chest, slamming him back against the door with such force that I heard a crack of wood. Beside me, Samuel bristled and his hand took mine, reassuring me that he would not let anything happen to me. I appreciated the gesture, although I wasn't scared. Jack's anger was directed at Patrick and the man looked terrified. He held up his hands in surrender.

"S-sorry, Jack, I meant no 'arm."

"Who you been sayin' that to?" Jack's voice was a low growl, just audible through the invading fog. "You don't know me no more," he went on. "Got that, Patrick? Now, tell me 'oo paid you to take them papers from Langley."

Patrick shook his head. "Can't say."

Jack slammed him back against the door again. The window nearby opened and the young boy's head popped out. "What's that racket?" When Jack glared at him, the lad ducked back inside and slammed the window shut.

"Tell me, Patrick," Jack snarled. "I ain't got time for this."

"I can't! Said 'e'd kill me if I told, 'e did."

"I'll bloody kill you if you don't." Two sparks flared in the darkness and one landed on Patrick's jacket. He yelped and patted it, and it quickly fizzled out.

"What was that?" Samuel whispered. "Did those sparks came from Jack's hands? Is he holding some sort of ignition device?"

"Whoa," said Patrick, breathing hard. "Careful, Jack-o'-lantern. It's just business. It ain't personal."

"It is to me." Jack's voice was once more cultured,

gentlemanly, but it was no less threatening. "They hang thieves."

"You wouldn't turn me in." Patrick's voice trembled. "We was friends once, don't that mean somethin' now?"

"Not if you cross me. Tell me who you work for, and I'll leave you alone. If you don't..." He patted the burned patch on Patrick's jacket. "I may not be able to control my temper next time."

Patrick's swallow could be heard clear across the street. "Don't tell 'im I told you."

"I won't."

"I don't know 'is name."

Jack's hands glowed but no sparks shot from them. "You must know something. Where can I find him? What does he look like?"

"I met 'im down at The Boar. Spoke like a toff, 'e did, and 'ad white 'air and only one arm."

"One arm?"

"Aye. And a shiny, pale face."

Jack nodded. "Anything else?"

"Nope. You goin' to the rozzers?"

"Not unless you do it again. Tommy begged me to keep your name to myself, for old time's sake."

Patrick grinned. "Them old times were a laugh, weren't they, Jack-o'-lantern? When you used to set stuff on fire—"

"Don't," Jack bit off. "Don't tell a soul about those days. Understand? My charity extends only so far."

Patrick nodded quickly. "Speakin' o' charity..." He jerked his head at the window where the lad had peeked out. "Winter's almost 'ere, and there's more comin' every day than I know what to do wiv."

"I'll send money and warm clothes as soon as I can. You only had to send word, Patrick. No need to take to thieving again."

"Once a thief, always a thief, eh, Jack-o'-lantern? We can't change 'oo we are deep down."

Jack stared at the window. "Don't lead any of those

children along that path. And don't steal from Langley again."

He strode toward us, and Samuel and I ducked further into the shadows as he passed. When I looked up again, Patrick had gone inside. The street was cold and quiet, the darkness almost complete except for the single lamp fading in and out near Patrick's door.

"Let's go," Samuel said. "Walk fast and don't make eye contact with anyone. We might just get out of here without being accosted."

I allowed him to lead me away as I considered what I'd just learned. One thing I was sure about now—Jack hadn't been involved in the theft of the papers from Langley. But I was even more certain that he was trying to deceive his so-called uncle by pretending to be his heir. As Patrick had said, Jack wasn't a Langley.

Someone reached out of the shadows and jerked me to a stop. I screamed and a hand clamped over my mouth. It stank, and I gagged into the palm. The other hand held a blade to my throat. It's cool metal bit into my skin but didn't cut.

Samuel stopped too. "Let her go," he said. His voice was steady, commanding. If he were afraid, he didn't show it. I, on the other hand, quivered like jelly.

"Give me yer money, sir, and she won't come to no 'arm."

"I haven't got any," Samuel said. "I gave it all away."

Brittle laughter filled my ear. Foul breath made me gag. I tried to shove the man off, but his grip tightened. *Oh God, Oh God, Oh God.*

"Then I want yer coat," he said.

Samuel removed his coat, and the attacker let go of my mouth to take it. But instead of handing it over, Samuel threw it. The man caught it, but he lowered the knife in that brief moment of confusion, and I ducked out of the way. Samuel stepped up and punched him in the nose. Blood sprayed over the coat and cobbles, but thankfully not on me.

Samuel grabbed my hand. We ran until we were out of the slum and back on the main street. We paused for breath within the circle of light cast by a lamp. I put a hand to my chest and sucked in air.

Samuel gripped my shoulders and searched my face. "Are you all right, Violet? Are you hurt?"

"No, I'm fine. Thank you, Samuel. You saved me."

His fingers kneaded my shoulders, but I got the feeling it was as much to reassure himself that I was unharmed than to comfort me. "I'm glad I was able to help."

I felt sick to my stomach. It was my fault entirely. He'd only agreed to accompany me because I'd insisted. What had I been thinking? "I'm so sorry, Samuel. I didn't know it would be like that. Those people...they're so...desperate."

"Starvation does that."

"I should have known. I've read the stories of Mr. Dickens."

He laughed and patted my hand. "Then you are indeed a woman of the world."

We walked off in what I assumed was the direction of Claridges, but in truth I couldn't be certain. The fog had become so thick it shrouded the entire street and I could see no landmarks, let alone recognize them. The *clip clop* of hooves and the rattle of wheels on the road signaled that a vehicle had gone past, but it could have been a spectral carriage for all I knew. It was nowhere to be seen. Behind us, footsteps echoed. I turned, but could see no one. The footsteps continued.

Had Jack doubled back and now followed us? Or had someone been following the entire time and I'd been too distracted to notice?

"I've just had a thought," Samuel said, apparently oblivious to the footsteps.

"Oh?" I looked back over my shoulder, but the *tap tap* of shoes on the pavement had ceased. "What about?" If it were about Jack, I already had a response in mind. I might not know everything about him, but I didn't want to divulge his fire-starting secret to Samuel. Not yet.

"Do you recall how you said your narcolepsy may be caused by fear?"

"Yes."

"I don't think it is, or you would have suffered an episode just now. You were terrified, weren't you?"

"More than I've ever been in my life." It was quite true, I realized. I'd not even been that afraid when I woke up in the carriage after Jack abducted me.

"Yet you didn't fall asleep."

"Good lord. You're right!"

"That means it has another trigger."

"Yes," I muttered. "Yes it does."

We reached the front door of Claridges, and a footman opened it for me. Before I had a chance to thank Samuel for his help and say goodbye, Sylvia barreled up and threw her arms around my neck.

"Thank goodness you're back," she said on a small sob. "I've been so worried."

"I sent word that I was going for a walk," I said.

She held me at arm's length. "Yes, but I knew you didn't know your way around London, and I've heard such dreadful things about girls getting lost and never being seen again." She smothered another sob with her hand. "I had a dim hope that you'd gone with Jack, but then he returned without you. We've been out of our minds with worry. Jack was just on his way out again to search for you."

Jack stood to one side in the foyer of the hotel. A desolate, bleak shadow passed across his face before he turned away, presenting me with a view of his back. He drew in several deep breaths and his fingers gripped the marble tabletop, his knuckles white.

"I'll speak to him," Samuel said.

"No!" Sylvia and I cried.

"Jack's temper is not to be trifled with," I added.

"He's not angry," Sylvia said, blinking at me. "He's as relieved as I am to have you back safely."

"In that case, perhaps I should be the one to speak to him." But I didn't get the chance. He strode off and up the stairs, taking two at a time. I sighed. "Perhaps tomorrow."

"Where did you go?" Sylvia asked.

"For a walk with Samuel."

She lifted a brow. "Samuel? I see. Well. I admit I thought a man of your profession would have better manners than to go walking in the dark with a young lady. I must admit, I'm very disappointed in you, Mr. Gladstone."

"Don't blame him," I said. "It was all my fault. I insisted."

"But...why? Where did you go?"

"Nowhere in particular. I needed some fresh air."

"Fresh air? In London?" Her gaze flicked to Samuel then back to me again. "I see."

"I'd better be on my way." Samuel bowed to both of us. "Good night, ladies. I'm glad I could be of service, Lady Violet."

"You were. Thank you, Samuel, from the bottom of my heart. Good bye."

He grinned and walked out the door. I hooked my arm through Sylvia's, and we headed for the stairs.

"Are you quite sure Jack isn't angry?" I asked. "He looked rather tempestuous just now."

"If he were angry, he'd have sparks spitting from his fingertips."

"I suppose so. Then why did he storm off without speaking to me?"

"Can't you see? He was sick with worry, then returned and it was obvious you'd spent the last little while walking with a man in the dark. A man that wasn't him."

"Oh." But there'd been something more in his eyes as he gazed at me. Not jealousy, but bitter disappointment too.

CHAPTER 9

Jack rode with Olson on the driver's seat on the way back to Hertfordshire, not inside the carriage cabin with Sylvia and me. I saw him only briefly when we arrived at Frakingham, and it wasn't until the next day when we were summoned to his uncle's rooms that we spoke.

"Jack, may we talk?" I said as he held the door open for me. "I don't like...this."

His jaw became a little less rigid, his eyes a little less vivid in color. "I hate it too. You and that Gladstone fellow..."

"It was just a walk, Jack, nothing more. I'm not interested in him in that way."

The muscles in his face relaxed. "Then—"

"Not now," Langley interrupted. "Both of you, come." He sat facing us, Bollard at his side like a guard dog. But it was the floor that caught my attention. Several small blackened scorch marks pockmarked the wood. They looked like they'd been put there by sparks that had been quickly doused. Jack must have done it when he and his uncle had argued over me being kept prisoner in the house a few days earlier. It was a shocking reminder that his temper was never far away, and of the damage it could cause.

"Is there anything you want to tell me, Jack?" Langley

asked.

"The hypnotist did indeed say Violet's memories were blocked, but he could do nothing to clear it," Jack said. "It was a wasted journey, I'm afraid. Sylvia, however, might say differently."

I smiled, and he winked at me. It was such a relief to be friends again.

"Nothing else?" Langley asked. At Jack's shrug, he added, "Is there something more you should be telling me?"

"No."

Langley heaved a great sigh. His face was pale and pinched, the wrinkles fanning out from the corners of his eyes deeper. "After everything I've done for you, everything I've given you, you lie to my face."

Jack's lips parted, and I heard him expel a small hiss. "What are you talking about?" His voice grew dark, ominous. He no longer looked at his uncle, but at me.

I frowned, shrugged, but a sense of dread settled in my chest. I knew what this was about. We both did.

"You saw someone while you were in London," Langley said. "An old friend of yours."

"And?"

"Don't treat me like a fool." He thumped his fist on the arm of his wheelchair. "He stole my papers, and *you* weren't going to tell me, or the police."

"I—"

"*Were you?*"

A muscle in Jack's cheek pulsed. "No."

"Why not?"

"I don't want him to get into trouble."

"It is not for you to make that decision!" Langley's shout reverberated around the room, and I jumped. I took a step back, not wanting to be anywhere near this man and his explosive temper.

Jack went very still, then slowly curled his fingers into a fist, but not before I noticed the tips glowing. "Patrick is not the one you want," he said.

"I know that."

He took a few breaths before saying, "I'm sure you do."

Langley's nostrils flared. "Dismissed. Both of you."

I hurried to the door, but Jack didn't move. "What are you going to do about Patrick?"

"He's a thief. He'll get what he deserves."

Jack leaned forward and clamped his hands down on the wheelchair arms, pinning Langley's hands. Bollard grabbed his shoulder and tried to pull him off, but Jack snarled at him and the servant backed away.

The expression on Langley's face changed from rage to horror to fear. "Let go!" he cried. "My hands...!"

Jack stepped back and Langley plunged his hands into a basin of water that Bollard had retrieved from the table near the window. Langley's eyelids fluttered shut in relief.

I covered my gasp and stared at Jack. Sparks flew from his fingertips and Bollard stamped on them before they could catch alight.

"Jack?" I whispered.

He seemed not to have heard me. His chest rose and fell with his seething anger, and he glared at his uncle. "Whatever you've done to Patrick, undo it. He's a pawn, and those children need him. If you don't...I won't remain here any longer."

He didn't wait to see if Langley agreed. He turned and fixed a glare on me that had me more confused than ever. His rage vanished almost instantly, replaced with such wretchedness that I wanted to reach for him. He blinked rapidly and hurried out of the room.

And that's when I realized he blamed me for telling his uncle about his visit to Patrick.

***

I searched for Jack everywhere. After checking with Olson at the stables, I found him at the abbey ruins, his horse grazing nearby. From a distance, he cut a lonely figure against the gray sky. He looked up when I approached and for a brief moment I was afraid he'd walk off in the other direction, but he didn't. He did, however, watch me with frightening intensity from beneath half-closed lids.

"You're still mad," I said.

He folded his arms and tucked away his hands, but not before I saw the pink flesh on his fingertips.

"I thought you said you could control your anger." I nodded at his hands. "And...that."

"I can."

Which meant he'd wanted to hurt Langley. And me? I swallowed heavily.

He unfolded his arms and his shoulders sagged. "You don't need to fear me, Violet. Not ever. I wouldn't deliberately hurt you."

"Then—"

"Why did you do it?" he asked. "Why did you tell him where I went?"

"So you did see me?"

"You and Gladstone. I lost you on the way home, however, so tell me...why?"

"I didn't tell him anything. What could I possibly gain?"

"Perhaps you're still angry at me for kidnapping you."

"I'm not. How could you think such a thing after..." *After the connection we'd made.* "Why didn't you tell me you'd seen me?"

"I hoped you'd talk to me of your own accord. But you didn't, and when August confronted me just now, I assumed you'd gone straight to him." He blew out a measured breath. "I'm sorry, Violet. Forgive me?"

I nodded. How could I not when he peered at me through the hair that had flopped over his eyes? He looked like a scolded puppy.

"So if it wasn't you," he said, "it must have been Gladstone."

"What reason would Samuel have to tell Langley? And how would he have gotten word to Frakingham so quickly?"

"So it's Samuel now, is it?"

"I call you Jack."

I wanted him to tell me that it was different between us, that the bond we'd forged so quickly *made* everything different. He did not.

"Why was he there at all?" he asked instead.

I decided it was better to be honest with him than skirt the issue. Well, partially honest. "He wanted to tell me that my memory block may have been deliberately put there by a hypnotist."

His jaw dropped. "Who would do such a thing?"

I told him what Samuel had told me about his own natural gift for hypnosis, and how he'd stumbled upon the ability by accident.

"What did Dr. Werner have to say about this suggestion?" Jack asked.

"He doesn't believe natural hypnotists exist, and so doesn't endorse the notion of deliberately blocking memories. That's why Samuel came to me at Claridges. He wanted to speak to me away from Dr. Werner."

He leaned against the stones that formed one of the crumbling arches. "It sounds too extraordinary to be true."

"So does shooting sparks from your fingers."

"Can Gladstone remove this block for you?"

"No. He thinks it can only be done through stimulating the same emotion that triggers my narcolepsy...and my fire starting. A very strong stimulation that is, more than usual."

"Hmmm."

"Hmmm? What does that mean?"

"It means that I'm not sure I entirely trust Samuel Gladstone. In many ways, the ability to hypnotize someone is far more dangerous than our talent. I admit that I don't like it."

"Don't like his talent or don't like him?"

His gaze slid away. "They're one and the same."

"So you still think he's the one who told your uncle?"

"Who else could have? I want to believe it wasn't you," he added in a whisper.

"It wasn't. I give you my word."

"Then it must have been him. A fast rider carrying a message would have easily reached Frakingham before us." He pushed off from the stones. "We should return to the house and resume your training."

"Is there any point now that we know about the blockage?"

"We can only keep trying."

He took his horse's reins, and we walked together back to the house. The gray clouds hung low overhead, and the air felt charged, thick, although that could have been due to the silence between us.

When I could stand it no longer, I said, "How do you know Patrick?"

"I just do."

"But—"

"Do you need to know everything, Violet?"

We'd reached the point where we needed to go our separate ways. He directed his horse off to the stables, and I headed for the main house. *Yes*, I wanted to tell him. *Yes, I do need to know everything about you.* Even though I couldn't tell him everything about myself. Not yet.

One day, however, he would know it all. And I would know every detail of Jack Langley's life, even if it meant finding out things I didn't like.

***

We trained for the remainder of the day. Jack tried various techniques to help me 'feel the heat' through my body, as he put it. Nothing worked, of course, and we ended our session at dinnertime. He seemed quite frustrated by our lack of progress, and I admit I was growing anxious about telling him the truth. The longer I lied, the harder it would be to admit that I wasn't Violet Jamieson and the worse his reaction would be.

I resolved to speak to Langley after dinner and confront him over his motives for kidnapping me. His reactions to a few direct questions should prove once and for all if he was lying about his intentions.

I dressed for dinner and met Sylvia and Jack in the dining room. She looked particularly lovely in a crimson and white gown with bows down the front and I told her so.

"This old thing," she said with a crinkle of her nose. "I'm so tired of it. Do you want it?"

"Thank you, but it's not my color."

"Perhaps not," she said, sitting. "I can't wait for our new dresses to arrive. Pity we don't have anything to wear them to except dinner with Jack."

"Something wrong with dining with me?" he asked as he too sat.

"You're hardly an excellent catch for either of us. Violet is the daughter of an earl and I am...more particular. No offense meant."

"And how could I take offense when you put it so eloquently?" It was difficult to tell if he were teasing or a little bitter.

"Perhaps you ought to ask some neighbors to a dinner party," I said.

Both Jack and Sylvia looked at me like I'd lost my mind. "Dinner at Freak House?" Sylvia said. "How they will be falling over themselves to attend."

"Why do they call this place Freak House? Do they know that Jack can start fires?"

"No," he said. "It's not that."

"It's Uncle August and Bollard." Sylvia served herself from the dish of Pheasant Mandarin that Tommy offered her. "One is mute and the other is crippled and...reclusive."

"August hasn't courted either the neighbors or the villagers so they distrust him," Jack said. "By secluding himself in the house, he's turned himself into an object of curiosity and gossip. I'm sure the servants have gossiped about his temper and how he keeps to his rooms."

"And there's the house's past, of course," Sylvia said.

"Its past?" I asked.

Jack cast a warning glare at Sylvia. "I'm not sure we need to hear this now."

"Nonsense. There are rumors that a hundred years or so ago, the then Lord Frakingham kept some of his offspring locked in the dungeon."

My stomach rolled. "Oh. How..." Familiar. "Horrid. Whatever for?"

"They were...imperfect," Jack said. "Due to centuries of inbreeding, it was said that most of the Frakingham children were born abnormal, some with physical deformities, others mad or simple."

"Freaks," I whispered.

Sylvia snorted as she picked at her pheasant. "It's not true. There is no dungeon. I've searched everywhere. Of course this house isn't as old as the stories. Who knows what the previous one on this site looked like. Perhaps it had a dungeon."

"The rumors have persisted anyway," Jack said.

What a strange coincidence that I should be kept in an attic almost my entire life only to be rescued, in a manner of speaking, and end up in a place where something similar occurred years earlier.

Over dinner, we discussed the viability of organizing a party with some of the well-to-do families in the area, but decided it had to be done with Langley's blessing. Sylvia was adamant she wouldn't have one without him present, and although Jack was less enthusiastic, he did agree that Langley should be kept informed.

His reaction only deepened my curiosity about his relationship with his uncle, if indeed that's what Langley was. While the two of them seemed to be in frequent conflict—and occasionally I was even convinced that Jack despised him—he always gave Langley due respect as master of the household. I admired him all the more for it.

Tommy brought out a dessert of jelly and served a portion to each of us, but when he got to Jack, he almost dropped the plate when Jack accidentally bumped him.

"Bloody hell, Tommy," Jack said, catching the footman's elbow to steady the plate.

"Sorry, Jackie. No harm done, eh?" He seemed to realize what he'd said as soon as the words left his mouth. He flushed and glanced at me. Jack pretended nothing was out of the ordinary and avoided my gaze altogether.

If I hadn't overheard their conversation a few nights earlier, I would have been confused by the informal exchange. It did get me thinking, however.

After dinner, I pretended I had a headache, but instead of retiring to my room, I went in search of Tommy in the service area. I found him in the large kitchen polishing a silver tray as the maids cleaned up after dinner. When they saw me, their chatter died and they stopped what they were doing.

"Lady Violet!" Tommy pushed back his chair to stand, toppling it over. "Is everything all right?"

"Yes, thank you. Tommy, is there somewhere we can talk?"

He covered a nervous little cough with his hand and led me to a sitting room nearby. Neither of us sat and he remained by the door, his hands behind his back, chin out. It was his footman's stance, the one he used when he stood in the dining room as we ate.

"Tommy, I have some questions for you."

"Yes, my lady."

"Tell me about the first time you met Jack."

There was a slight twitching of muscle in his cheek, a faltering of his steady gaze. "I can't rightly remember, my lady."

"I know you knew him before he came to Frakingham."

He blinked, but said nothing.

"I know that Jack came from a London slum, and that you did too. What I don't know, and what I want you to tell me, is what led him here."

"I couldn't say."

The man was loyal, I'd give him that. "Why are you protecting him?"

"He don't need my protection. But a man is entitled to

his privacy, ma'am. If he don't want you to know about his past, then I've got no right to tell you."

"If he didn't want *me* to know?" I stepped up to him. He was much taller than me, but not as tall as Jack. "Why not *me* specifically?"

Sweat beaded on his brow, yet he didn't answer.

"If you don't tell me, Tommy, I'm afraid I'll have to go to Mr. August Langley and inform him that you knew about Patrick breaking into the house too. I doubt he'll be pleased to hear that. He might not throw his nephew out, but I doubt his mercy will extend to you. Do you like your job here?"

Tommy gawped slack-jawed at me. "You...you'd chirp to Mr. Langley?"

"I don't want to." I turned away, so he couldn't see me cringe as I lied. "But if I had to..."

"Bloody hell," Tommy muttered. "He'll kill me."

I wasn't sure whether he meant Jack or Langley. "I won't tell either of them what is said between us now. It'll be our secret."

He muttered something under his breath then sighed. "Promise you won't tell Jack I said this."

"I promise."

His body lost some of its stiffness, as if he'd decided to shed his footman persona and put on his real one. "His name's Jack Cutler, not Langley. I met him when he came to join our family."

"Family?"

"Not a real one, but that's what our little group called ourselves. We were orphans, him and me. Patrick too, and some others. We looked after one another. We had to or we'd starve to death, or be taken by the rozzers and be sent to the workhouses. Or worse."

"Worse than the workhouses?" I'd heard about the terrible conditions of workhouses. How the food was riddled with maggots, the beds and clothes with lice, and the children forced to work inhuman hours or suffer a beating.

"There were Haymarket Hectors out to get boys and girls like us," he said. "Prostitution," he clarified when I shook my head.

Oh my God. I felt sick to my stomach, and suddenly so very lucky that I'd only had to endure the solitude of an attic for fifteen years. There was much worse out there for orphans. I'd been fortunate, as had Jack, Tommy and their friends.

"We got by," Tommy said. "Stealing mostly, sometimes finding work doing the jobs no one else wanted. We never froze in winter though. Jack and his...fingers saw to that. Then that big mute comes up and hands Jack a letter one day. Jack can't read, so he takes it to the baker down the street who can. The letter says he's the nephew of August Langley and that he wanted to adopt him."

"And then?"

Tommy shrugged. "Then he came here, bringing me with him. Langley didn't want me though, so he made me a footman because Jack says he's not staying if I don't too. He's a good friend. Like a brother. We've always taken care of each other."

"So...*is* he August Langley's nephew? You said his name was Cutler, but now he goes by Langley."

Tommy shrugged. "Maybe he is, maybe he isn't. All I know is, the old man gave Jack an education, horses, an allowance. Why would he be so generous if he weren't a relation?"

"I suppose." Yet it didn't make sense. According to Sylvia, there'd been three Langley brothers—her father, Jack's father, and August himself. Yet Jack had been a Cutler not a Langley. And what of Tommy's and Patrick's doubts on the matter?

I thought about asking him if Jack had a more nefarious motive for staying, but decided not to. He was as loyal to Jack as he could be, and if he did know anything, I was sure he'd deny it.

"Thank you, Tommy. I'm sorry to have put you through

this."

He sighed. "I suppose it had to come out sooner or later. You'll keep your promise, won't you, m'lady? You won't tell Jack you and me spoke?"

"I won't. Are you afraid of him?"

"No, but I don't want him to be disappointed in me. He trusts me, and that's the way I want it to stay."

I squeezed his arm and he dipped his head, but not before I saw his cheeks redden. "Don't worry, I won't say anything. Believe me, I understand what it's like to have Jack disappointed in me."

He blinked. "You do?"

I nodded. "I followed him in London when he went to see Patrick. He thought I told Langley about the meeting, but I wouldn't tell that man anything if I could help it."

His frown drew his thick brows together into a single line. "I think I know who it was who told Mr. Langley."

"Who?"

"Bollard."

I gasped. "How do you know?"

"I can't be sure, but he left Frakingham just after you and got back just before. Maybe he went to London."

I nodded slowly. "Perhaps he did. Do you think he might have followed Jack too and overhead the conversation?"

"P'haps."

"But surely I would have noticed." And yet, I *had* heard footsteps following us, although not until we were almost back at Claridges. It was entirely possible that I was too distracted earlier to hear them.

"He can read lips, you know," Tommy said.

"Bollard? I thought he was a mute, not deaf."

He shrugged. "He's not deaf, but I know he can read lips like a deaf person. I wouldn't put it past him to have told Mr. Langley what he saw and heard."

"No. Nor would I."

CHAPTER 10

Bollard opened the door on my knock and gave a formal, curt bow. When he straightened, he raised his eyebrows in question, but did not step aside.

"I need to speak to Mr. Langley," I said.

"She may enter," came Langley's voice from within.

Bollard opened the door wider and I went through. It took me a moment to realize Langley wasn't in the immediate part of the room furnished as a parlor, but in the end that served as a laboratory. He sat at a low table, his head bent over a microscope.

"Mr. Langley, I—"

He held up his forefinger for silence, and I dutifully shut my mouth, biting my tongue in the process. I waited as he wrote something down then wheeled his chair out and turned to look at me.

"I'm glad you've come to see me, Violet," he said. "We need to speak about London again. It'll be easier without Jack here." He moved his chair forward, pushing the wheels with his hands. It looked arduous and progress was slow until Bollard rescued him. Once he was near me, Langley indicated I should sit.

"Refreshments, Bollard," he said. When the servant

hesitated, he added in a softer voice, "I'll be all right."

Bollard left, but the exchange piqued my curiosity. It was almost as if Bollard's concern went beyond that of a master for his servant. I supposed they'd been together a long time, and Bollard did do more than a mere valet or laboratory assistant. He was Langley's legs too, and, it seemed, his eyes and ears. Why he thought I'd hurt Langley was a mystery though.

"I'm sorry the hypnotist couldn't help," Langley said. "Truly sorry. We'll have to continue your training. Is Jack making progress?"

"A little," I hedged.

"Good. It was a shame you had to witness his temper, Violet. Jack can be very...passionate. I do hope you realize that it was entirely directed at me and had nothing to do with you."

"Why does he dislike you so?"

He rubbed the palm of his hands along the arms of his wheelchair. "You would have to ask him that."

"I find it strange considering you rescued him from the streets and have given him a comfortable life here at Frakingham. Shouldn't he be grateful?"

"To repeat: you should be asking him."

"I followed him into the slums of London, although I suspect you know that already." He blinked slowly and I took that as confirmation. "He knew his way in the darkness, which is remarkable since my escort and I got lost on the way back to Claridges."

"What are you getting at, Violet?"

It was difficult to speak of the matter without implicating Tommy. I needed to tread carefully. "Is Jack originally from that very slum where he met the man named Patrick?"

He didn't answer.

"He's not your nephew, is he?"

"Isn't he?"

"Mr. Langley, I have agreed to remain here until Christmas, against my better judgment. If you continue to evade sensible questions, then I may not be able to keep that promise." I don't know where I got the courage to speak so boldly to such a man as August Langley. The fact that I had seemed to trouble him less than me. I swallowed and hoped I hadn't overstepped the mark.

"If you want to find out about Jack's past, ask *him*. Now, if you came here to waste my time then we're finished. You may go. It seems we don't have much to say to one another after all." He shifted his wheelchair backwards, away from me. He was dismissing me as casually as he'd dismissed Bollard. It irked me that he could disregard such an important point.

I stood abruptly and caught the arm of his chair. "I am asking *you*, Mr. Langley." I suddenly wasn't afraid of him anymore. What could a crippled man do to me? If Bollard were there it may be a different matter, but he wasn't. If Langley turned me out, I'd return to Windamere. "Is Jack your blood relative?"

"Let go of my chair, Violet."

"Answer me, Mr. Langley."

He caught my sleeve and dragged me down to his level. His face was a distorted mask of anger, his mouth a twisted gash. "*You* do not tell *me* what to do."

Something inside me shattered, and I jerked free of his grip. I did not step back. I did not look away or run for the door. I would not fear this man, nor would I endure any more of his lies and threats. If I wanted to walk away, I would. I had been kept prisoner at Windamere for fifteen years. I'd been denied a life, and even if that life had turned out to be a dire, desperate one, at least it would have been mine to make of it what I could.

I'd had enough of being told what to do and how to conduct myself. Enough of being told to accept my condition and situation, that I ought to consider myself lucky. I wasn't lucky. I was a prisoner, and I'd be damned if I would endure it on anyone else's terms anymore, especially someone as nasty as Langley.

"You let Jack think I told you about his visit to Patrick," I said, choosing the one thing I knew the answer to. The one thing I could absolutely blame him for without a doubt. "Why? Why didn't you tell him it was Bollard?"

His lips peeled back and he bared his teeth. "I already told you I don't answer to you." He spat out each word as if they were poison on his tongue. "Your father may be an earl, but here, that means nothing. You're nobody. Your opinion means nothing, your questions even less. You are our prisoner, and I do *not* answer your questions."

His voice rang in my ears, throbbed in my veins. My blood rose like a tidal wave, rushed through me, fast and fierce. Hot. It was so loud that I hardly heard the door open, but I turned just in time to see Jack enter, Bollard at his heels.

"No!" Jack shouted. His brows crashed together in a deep frown. "Stop it, August. Are you mad?" Sparks flew from his fingers onto the floor, but he quickly stomped them out as he approached us. "Tell her she's not a prisoner. Tell her she can come and go. *Tell her!*"

Langley laughed, the sound like fingernails down a blackboard. "Of course she can't leave. You know that as well as I do."

"Jack!" I cried. "Is that true?"

But Jack's gaze was fixed on his uncle. It was filled with such fury that I was amazed his fingers didn't explode. "I will not be a party to this." His voice was quiet, cold, and filled me with dread.

"You can't leave, Violet," Langley said. "Jack has known this all along. He's been keeping an eye on you. Lying to you. We all have."

Everything dimmed, and I thought I was going to fall asleep at the worst possible moment, but then my vision cleared, only to see sparks spraying around the room like fireworks. So many of them. Too many.

They landed on the curtain, the floor, the table and even in Langley's lap. He yelped and swatted them just as the curtain went up in a *whoosh* of flames. Some of the furniture had caught alight, the floorboards too.

We had to get out.

"My research!" Langley cried, wheeling himself toward the laboratory.

"Not now!" Jack cried. "Bollard!"

Bollard rushed past me, and I stumbled forward, my body suddenly heavy, my head filled with cotton wool. Jack caught me and picked me up. We didn't combust. That was something. I was a rag doll in his arms. Exhaustion dragged at me, pulling me into a slumber. But I did not fall asleep.

"Get out!" Jack shouted. "Forget the papers!"

But Bollard didn't listen. He scooped up some notebooks and stuffed them into his jacket, then he returned and picked up Langley. They followed us to the door, but flames were already licking up the doorframe. Wood cracked and popped in the heat, and I felt that I might do the same. I burned as if I had a fever.

Jack held me tighter then ran through the doorway onto the landing. "Tommy!" he shouted. "Water!"

My head bumped against Jack's shoulder as he ran down the stairs, giving orders to the servants to put out the flames. "Don't endanger yourselves."

He carried me outside where the crisp evening air slammed against my hot face. It was raining and I was so glad I almost cried. The rain would help put the fire out. Bollard and Langley followed us, and the female servants weren't far behind, carrying silver and other valuables. Sylvia wasn't among them.

"We have to find her," I said, clawing at Jack's shirt.

He glanced down at me. He seemed shocked to see me still awake. "I'll do it," he said, but as he set me gently on the ground, Tommy ran out of the house, Sylvia tucked into his side.

He brought her to us, and she flopped down beside me and drew me into a hug. She sobbed against my throat.

I held her close, so relieved she was all right. She was

shaking and crying, but seemed unharmed.

Tommy and Jack raced off to join the male servants fighting the fire. Smoke billowed out of the windows and rose into the wet night. I heard Jack give orders to protect the rest of the house, and I closed my eyes and prayed for the first time in a long time. I just hoped God remembered me and listened.

"Sylvia?" said Langley. He was still in Bollard's arms. The servant held him as if he weighed nothing and seemed in no mind to put him down. "Sylvia, are you harmed?"

She shook her head and wiped her cheeks. "I'm all right, Uncle. I'd gone to bed early, but Tommy rescued me. If he hadn't..." She sobbed again and I circled her shoulders with my arm. "He's so brave."

"It will all be over soon," I said, eyeing the top floor of the house. "Perhaps I should go and help."

"No!" Sylvia and Langley cried.

"Stay here with me," Sylvia said. "Let the men do it."

"But I ought to help."

"It's not your fault," Langley said. He sounded surprisingly humble and kind. There was none of the anger and taunting of earlier. The fire must have shocked him into sensitivity. It must certainly be a shocking thing to watch as one's house went up in flames.

"I know that," I said. "But I don't like to do nothing when I'm needed."

"There's a well out the back and a pump and hoses stored in the service area for just such an emergency. They'll cope without you."

It was a long way from the service area to the well and up to Langley's rooms, but I didn't say so.

Sylvia held my hand and snuggled closer. Her body shook. She must have been freezing in her nightshift and shawl. I tried to keep her warm by rubbing her arms and feet, but her shaking didn't subside even when one of the maids brought her a blanket.

It seemed to take all night for the fire to die down

completely, but in truth it was probably less than an hour. From where we sat on the front lawn, it was clear that Langley's room had been destroyed, but beyond that, we couldn't tell.

When Jack joined us, Sylvia was half asleep against me. She leapt to her feet as he approached and ran to him. "Where's Tommy? Is he all right?"

"Everyone's fine." Jack wiped the back of his hand across his brow, smearing it with soot.

"The house?" Langley said. Bollard had held him the entire time and still did not look as if he wanted to put him down.

"The eastern wing may be unstable, but the service area and rest of the house are fine."

"But our rooms are on the eastern side," Sylvia said, pulling the blanket to her chin. "Where shall we go?"

"We'll open up the southern wing," Langley said. "Come, before we freeze to death."

Bollard led the way with Langley in his arms. Sylvia and I followed, Jack behind us. I heard him question each of the servants, asking if they were all right, reassuring the frightened maids that the fire would not flare again.

"Boil as much water as you can as quickly as you can," Jack told the housekeeper, Mrs. Moore. "Bring water bottles and hot tea to the parlor in the southern wing then see to your own comfort. Everyone is to avoid the eastern wing until further notice."

"But none of the rooms are ready in the southern wing, sir," said Mrs. Moore.

"Prepare rooms for the ladies and Mr. Langley. I'll remain in the parlor until the morning."

We skirted the front of the house and the housekeeper unlocked a side door with one of the keys hanging at her waist. We followed Bollard and Langley into a small room that smelled musty and stale, with only a hint of lingering smokiness. Pale mounds loomed out of the darkness, but as my eyes adjusted, I realized they were dust sheets covering the furniture. Nothing hung on the wood-paneled walls, not even wallpaper. It was a cheerless, bland room.

Jack lit two candles on the mantel with a single touch of his forefinger, while Sylvia and I whipped off the sheets. Bollard finally lowered Langley onto one of the chairs and stretched the muscles in his arms. Tommy entered carrying wood and a box of kindling. A maid trailed behind, laden with hot water bottles. Sylvia grabbed one and cuddled it to her chest. He watched as Tommy set the wood box down.

"You're a savior," she said to him. Tommy smiled sheepishly and dipped his head. Sylvia appeared not to see him blush as she blew on her bare hands. "It's freezing in here."

Tommy placed the wood in the grate and Jack lit the fire. Sylvia sighed and spread her fingers in front of the flickering flames. "That's better," she muttered.

"Go get some rest, Tommy," Jack said. "You deserve it."

"But you need—"

"Never mind us," Langley said. "Mrs. Moore will bring in the tea and we can serve ourselves."

Tommy left and silence blanketed our little group. I watched the flames flicker around the wood, their dance seductive as they ate their fill. We all seemed mesmerized by it, but I for one felt quite sick. The fire had destroyed part of the house, and it had almost destroyed us too. If we hadn't got out of Langley's rooms...

I shuddered to think what may have happened.

I glanced at Jack and was startled to see that he was watching me. He offered a small smile, but I didn't return it. The shock of what he'd done was too fresh. His anger was far more volatile than I'd thought, and more dangerous. He'd said he could control it, but clearly he could not.

And of course, I knew now that he'd lied to me all along. There'd never been any agreement to let me go at Christmas. Langley had intended to keep me prisoner no matter what. And Jack knew it.

Langley also watched me, but with a gravity that was at

odds with his earlier nastiness. Ever since then, he'd been quiet, reflective, and not at all the confrontational man I'd come to expect.

Mrs. Moore entered with a tray of tea things and left us to serve ourselves. Sylvia poured and handed out cups. She drank hers quickly and gave a deep sigh, then refilled it from the pot.

"Well, this is awkward," she said, setting the pot down with a loud clank. "Would someone care to tell me what caused the fire? I take it that one of you couldn't control yourselves," she said with a pointed glare at first me then Jack.

When neither Jack nor Langley answered, I said, "Your uncle said something rather shocking to me. Something that Jack didn't want me to know."

You can't leave, Violet.

The words sliced through me like a blade. I sucked in a breath to try to steady my nerves, but it was no use. Unlike earlier, I wasn't angry anymore. That moment had passed. Now...now, I was terrified.

"What didn't Jack want you to know?" Sylvia looked so innocent, so untouched and honest. Yet she knew the truth too. She and her cousin—if that's what he was—were part of Langley's plan to keep me prisoner at Freak House.

"It's not important," Langley said. "The important thing is that you didn't fall asleep, Violet. You were close, weren't you, but you didn't. It's a triumph."

"Is that what that was all about?" Jack said. A thread of steel ran through his otherwise calm voice. "That's low, August. Even for you."

"Will someone tell me what's going on?" Sylvia asked. "Who set the house on fire? Violet?"

"Yes," Jack said at the same time that I said, "No."

He blinked at me. Langley lowered his cup to his saucer. "You don't know?" he murmured.

"All I know is that you are a pack of wolves and I despise you. If I must stay here, then I will, but I will not be a party to your charade. I'll not pretend all is well. You'll have to lock me up if you wish to keep me here." My voice shook. My hands too and I had to set the cup down lest the tea spill.

"Violet?" Sylvia was at my side, crouching on the floor near my feet. Her gaze searched mine before she turned it on Langley. "What have you said to her, Uncle?"

"Wait." Jack held up his hand. He shook his head, his brow deeply furrowed. "Tell us what happened up there, Violet. What happened within you, I mean."

"I'll not tell you a thing," I snapped. "If you and your mad uncle wish to learn anything about me, you'll have to dissect my cadaver in his laboratory. I'm sure it'll give you much pleasure."

"Violet, stop," he whispered, kneeling in front of me beside his cousin. "It's not what you think."

"Isn't it? You heard him as clearly as I did. I'm a prisoner, and you and your cousin are aiding him. You are a liar, a kidnapper and much more besides."

"What?" Sylvia straightened. "That's ridiculous. We have an agreement. You're to stay until Christmas, but then you're free to go. You're certainly not a prisoner."

"Wait, Syl." Jack laid a hand on her arm, but he continued to stare at me. "You got angry, Violet. Remember? You were furious with August and me, perhaps more than you've ever been in your life. You felt tired, and usually you would fall asleep, but not this time. This time you stayed awake, so you know what happened next. You *know*, Violet. Remember?"

His melodic voice soothed me somewhat and tears welled in my eyes. How could he have lied to me? After his kindness, his affection. "I believed you," I whispered as tears spilled down my cheeks. "I trusted you." Sylvia reached for me and I pushed her away. "Both of you."

"How *could* you?" Sylvia wailed at Langley.

Her uncle sat stoically, unmoved.

"Tell me what happened next, Violet," Jack said, his voice urgent. "The sparks. Do you remember those?"

"This is absurd," I muttered. "Very well, if you want to

relive it then I'll recount the events. You grew angry with your uncle because you didn't want him to tell me what was really going on—that I am a prisoner and you all know it. It seems you couldn't control your temper this time, Jack. Perhaps you're the one who needs training, not me." I sounded bitter, but I didn't care. My energy had leached from me, and I was too tired to play their game. It was the truth or nothing. They were mad and I truly was their prisoner.

But not forever. I would escape and warn Violet. They couldn't be allowed to win. There was only one way to beat them, and that was admit the truth, or part of it. I would not admit it all and put Vi in danger.

"No, Violet," Langley said, his thick brows plunging into a frown. "You're incorrect. It wasn't Jack. It was you."

"Impossible," I snapped.

"You'd better explain why," Jack said.

"I can't start fires, you see. I never could." There. I'd said it and I felt relieved beyond measure. They'd not want me now that they knew I was of no use to them. All I had to do was convince them that Vi couldn't do it either and they'd just let me go. Dear God.

Jack sat back on his haunches. "Yes," he said, reaching for me then pulling away. "You can. August, Bollard and I just witnessed it. Those sparks didn't come from me. They came from you. Don't you remember?"

My laughter came out harsh, but even as my head thought he was lying, my heart knew the reality. It drummed out a different tune in my chest. It was time I listened.

He was right. I was a fire starter.

CHAPTER 11

"Violet?" Jack's soft voice startled me out of my foggy stupor. "Violet? Are you telling us you didn't know?"

"How could she not know?" asked Sylvia.

How indeed.

Her face appeared in front of mine, her big eyes filled with concern. "Are you all right, Violet? You look very pale."

I gripped the chair arms until my fingers ached, but I didn't let go. If I did, I was sure I would tip over. My thoughts raced so fast I couldn't quite grasp them. All I knew was that if I could start fires, then everyone at Windamere had lied to me.

Including Vi.

"Violet?" Jack still knelt in front of me, so close I could feel the heat radiating from him. It made my skin hot, my blood hotter.

Or was that the heat within me? It all began to make sense. I'd never felt cold, never needed a coat to go outside and I hated wearing gloves. Where Vi had shivered through our wintry walks, I'd relished the cold breeze against my skin, the frost in the air.

"Do you need to lie down?" he asked me.

I shook my head. "I need...answers."

"Whatever we can provide, we will." He took a deep breath and scrubbed his hand over his jaw.

"Why did you lie to us?" Langley said. "You let us believe you could start fires even though you thought you couldn't."

"Don't," Jack warned. "Our questions can wait. Let Violet ask hers first."

Langley heaved a deep sigh. "Very well. I suppose you'd like to know what happened up there."

I nodded.

"Bollard told me what the Gladstone fellow told you."

"*Bollard* followed us!" Jack snapped. "Bloody hell, August. Why?"

"I originally sent him to London to make sure Violet didn't escape." He gave a jerky nod of apology. "I didn't quite trust her." At Jack's protest, he put up his hand and continued over the top of him. "He followed all three of you when you visited your friend. Bollard's deaf mother taught him to read lips, and he used the skill in order to keep his distance. He missed some of the conversations thanks to the poor light, but he caught most. As well as the meeting you had with your friend, he told me everything the Gladstone fellow told Violet."

"What did he tell her?" Sylvia clicked her tongue. "And why am I always the last to know?"

"Gladstone informed Violet that her narcolepsy could be cured by subjecting her to a profound dose of the emotion that triggers it."

"But we didn't know what that emotion was," Jack said.

"I suspected it was anger. I always did. That first time she unexpectedly fell asleep here and almost set my laboratory on fire, her temper was pronounced."

"The first time...?" I whispered. "There...there was a fire? Why didn't anyone tell me?" I remembered the fresh scorch marks on Langley's floor that hadn't been there upon my first visit...I'd thought Jack had put them there. That was me?

Jack and Langley looked askance. "We merely assumed you'd been aware of what happened that day," Jack said. "It never occurred to me to discuss the incident in detail. Wait a moment." He turned to Langley. "I see now. You lied to her about not being able to leave because you *wanted* her to get angry. You let her think Sylvia and I were in on the trickery."

"What do you mean?" Sylvia stamped a hand on her hip. "Once again I'm the last to know everything."

"I had no choice," Langley said to Jack, ignoring her. He shrugged, as if it were nothing. As if manipulating my emotions and making me believe Jack lied didn't matter, as long as he got the outcome he wanted.

The heat rose within me again, but not enough to produce sparks or flames. Unlike Jack. He looked like he wanted to set something alight. His breathing had become ragged, his nostrils flared. At least there were no sparks.

"What happened in your room, Uncle?" Sylvia asked.

Jack gave a low, bitter laugh. "Our dear Uncle August knew that anger would cure Violet of her narcolepsy and was also the trigger that would ignite the heat inside her. He decided to set up a little experiment."

"Not an experiment," Langley said. "An experiment is where you test a hypothesis within a controlled environment. I bypassed the experiment and went straight to administering the cure."

Sylvia gasped. "Good lord. Was that wise?"

"I think we all saw how *unwise* it was," Jack muttered.

"Now it makes sense," Sylvia said. "You deliberately made her angry with a lie about her being kept prisoner here. Uncle, how *could* you?"

"Enough! I did what was necessary to remove the narcolepsy and memory block. Now we can start her training anew."

I pressed my fingers to my temples. My head ached. My heart was sore. I should be disturbed by Langley's admission, but I couldn't muster any thoughts in that direction. All I knew was that Vi and Miss Levine had lied to me for many years. My world had been turned upside down and shaken about. I felt like I was watching a grand illusionist working his magic so cleverly and subtly that the sleight of hand went unnoticed. Nothing was as it seemed anymore.

"I think you need to lie down," Jack said, once more crouching in front of me. He peered at me as if he would see my thoughts. It was clear from his earnest gaze that he wanted to hold me, just as I wanted to be held by him. But touching of an intimate nature was impossible. He may have been able to carry me to safety, but there'd been no desire in his touch then, only urgency.

It would seem that anger caused me to light fires, but mutual desire caused us both to combust.

"I'll find out if the maids have made up any of the bedrooms," Sylvia said.

"Wait." Langley tapped his finger on the arm of his chair. "You owe me an explanation, Violet."

"She doesn't," Jack growled.

"It's all right," I said. "I want to tell you." I needed to, if only to help me make sense of it.

"Why did you not tell us you thought you couldn't light fires?" Langley asked. "If you didn't want to stay here, why not inform us of what you thought was the truth?"

Three sets of eyes watched me intently. Only Bollard seemed disinterested. I sucked in a breath and let it out slowly before beginning. "I was protecting my friend. I thought she was the fire starter, not me. She's not as strong as me, you see. She scares easily and I wanted to protect her from...your experiments. If your intentions truly were to do harm or to study her then I wanted to keep her safely at Windamere."

"That's so sweet of you," Sylvia said, sniffing and dabbing at the corners of her eyes.

"She's lucky to have a friend like you," Jack said.

"Except we're not friends, are we?" I said, bitterness souring my tongue. "How can we be? She's been lying to me for years. She knew I was the one who started the fires, yet she allowed me to think it was her and that my narcolepsy was somehow tied to it." I shook my head. It sounded ridiculous now that I thought about it. Why would *my* narcolepsy have been caused by *her* being able to start fires, or vice versa?

"Why would she do that?" Langley asked.

"Yes," Jack said. "Why lie at all?"

I shrugged. I felt like the stupidest fool that ever lived. "I don't know. They were all lying. Miss Levine, Lord Wade and Violet—"

"Violet?" Jack frowned. "But you're Violet?"

I chewed the inside of my cheek and tasted blood. "My name is Hannah Smith."

Langley's fingers gripped his chair arms. "Hannah...Smith," he muttered.

"You've heard of me?"

He lifted a hand in dismissal, but the distance in his eyes remained.

"You're not the daughter of Lord Wade?" Jack asked.

"No. Violet Jamieson, my friend, is. I was her companion, confined to the attic alongside her because she couldn't be let out with her condition." I twisted my hands together, knotting the fingers. "Or so I thought. But since I am the fire starter, and she isn't...I don't understand why Lord Wade kept me at all. Or why she's in the attic."

"Who are your parents?" Jack asked.

"Lord Wade's servants. They died when I was a baby."

"I'm terribly confused," Sylvia said. "Are we to address you as Hannah now?"

I nodded.

"You're not a lord's daughter?"

"No."

"You're a...*servant*?"

"A lady's companion." Which was little better. "Shall I remove myself to the servant's quarters?" I asked, unable to keep my snide tone in check.

"No," Langley said before the others could speak. "You're our guest as much now as you were when we thought we had Lady Violet. That doesn't change. Sylvia, go see if the maids are finished making up the rooms. Hannah needs some rest. We all do."

"I didn't mean anything by it," Sylvia muttered as she left.

"You told me that Lady Violet was the one with red hair," Jack said to Langley. His eyes narrowed, as if he were deep in thought trying to solve a puzzle. "They both had red hair, although different shades."

"I wasn't to know that," Langley said.

"So why take me and not the real Violet Jamieson?" I asked Jack. "You saw us both, yet you kidnapped me. Why?"

He shook his head, frowning. "I...I was led to believe..."

"Believe what?"

He paused before answering, and I got the feeling whatever he was about to tell me wasn't the entire truth. "I watched you both during your walks. You seemed to be the one in charge. You led, she followed. You were feisty where she was meek. I assumed that meant you were the earl's daughter and that the earl's daughter was the fire starter. Besides," the corner of his mouth lifted in a fleeting smile, then it vanished and he looked down at his feet, "I felt a strong connection to you. Like I was being tugged toward you by an invisible leash." He looked up again and our gazes locked. My spine tingled and heat flared through my body. "Why would I feel that unless you were a fire starter too?" He shrugged. "I didn't question it."

A tug toward me. Because of my ability or because he desired me? He smiled again, a soft, knowing smile that I desperately wanted to capture. Knowing it was just for me would have to be enough.

"Will you teach me to control this?" I asked.

The smile turned achingly sad. "I hope so. It should be a matter of controlling your temper. But unless you can turn off...more intimate emotions at will, then I'm afraid I can't help you when we..." He cleared his throat. "Just as I cannot help myself. I will find a cure though. I promise you, V— Hannah."

I gave an emphatic nod. I no longer needed any

convincing to stay at Frakingham. There was nothing for me at Windamere anymore, and everything at Freak House. "We'll find it together," I said.

***

I slept fitfully in a bedroom I shared with Sylvia. The following morning, she peppered me with questions over breakfast in the parlor. What was the real Lady Violet like? How could I not know I was a fire starter? And, the one that confused me most—why had Lord Wade kept me at all? The only explanation I could come up with was that there was something wrong with Vi. There had to be some reason he'd keep his daughter in the attic with me, away from public view.

As I listened to Sylvia's chatter and ate my eggs, I questioned not only my reason for being confined at Windamere, but also my reason for leaving it. Jack had been hiding something when he spoke of kidnapping me and not Vi. I'd noticed his hesitations, yet he'd smoothed out the wrinkles in his story so expertly that I'd failed to recall my unease until now. I would have asked him except he'd eaten breakfast an hour earlier according to Tommy, and had since disappeared.

I went in search of Langley instead. He'd taken his breakfast in his new temporary room along the corridor from my bedroom. I knocked and Bollard opened the door. The big servant filled the doorway, his presence as solid and imposing as ever. If he felt guilty for following me in London and playing a part in the fire, he didn't show it.

Langley sat in a chair at a small desk facing the center of the room. A collection of blackened equipment filled a box nearby, and he was pouring over half-burnt pieces of paper. Bollard must have gathered up anything that was salvageable from the laboratory and brought them to the new room.

"Was much of your research destroyed?" I asked.

"Some." He didn't sound nearly as annoyed as I thought he would be. I'd come prepared with a speech that put the blame for the fire back onto him. Considering he'd deliberately riled me, I thought it only fair he acknowledged his role. It seemed unnecessary now, and perhaps a little petty when he didn't seem too upset.

"How are you this morning, Hannah?"

"Well enough, considering I've just learned that I'm not who I thought I was."

"That's a dramatic way of putting it."

"You try going from being a narcoleptic to a fire starter in one evening. It would be like..." I searched for a metaphor and settled on the obvious. "Like suddenly discovering that you can walk again."

"Not necessarily a bad thing."

"Sorry." I chewed my lip, but he smiled. It was so unexpected and out of character that my jaw flopped open.

"Sit, Hannah. I suspect you have questions."

"Several, but I don't think you can answer them all. How did I get to be a fire starter? Was I born this way?"

"You're right, I can't answer them all."

Can't or won't? I sighed and flounced onto the chair, only to have to reposition myself on the edge of the seat when the bustle in the back of my dress got in the way.

"Would you like to speak to Lord Wade?" he asked.

I stared open-mouthed at him. "Me speak to Lord Wade?" I snorted. "The man hasn't said a word to me in all the time I've known him. Why would he deign to talk to me now?"

"I could arrange a meeting."

"In his house?"

He shrugged one shoulder. "Do you want to go back there?"

"I'd like to speak to Vi. I'd like to ask her..." I choked back a sob that had unexpectedly risen to my throat. "I'd like to ask her why she lied to me all this time."

"Perhaps she was told to."

I contemplated that for a moment. She had lied to me for years, even as a child. It must have been an order from the earl. Vi was my friend. We'd cared for one another, laughed together and cried together. She'd never have willingly lied. My feelings toward her tempered somewhat, although not entirely.

The day of the kidnap came back to me. Her nervousness had been more pronounced than ever, and I'd had the very strong feeling that she *was* keeping something from me. At the time, I'd thought she wanted me to stay away from the mysterious gardener—Jack—but now...now I wondered if she were pushing me toward him, albeit reluctantly.

Miss Levine had also been on edge that day, and yet eager for us to go for a walk despite the looming storm. She'd also disappeared very quickly when it began to rain and not followed us into the woods. The woods that Vi *had* wanted to enter when usually she hated it.

Had they known I was about to be kidnapped? Known and...wanted it?

I felt sick. I couldn't breathe. *Vi... how could you?*

"Put your head between your knees, Hannah. Breathe."

Bollard's strong hand gently pressed the back of my neck, pushing me forward so that I folded up on myself. I breathed deeply until the nausea vanished and my head cleared. I felt ill all over again, not because Vi had colluded with Miss Levine to force me into a trap, but because it was Jack who'd orchestrated the trap. He must have, or how would they know to lead me into the woods? He'd enlisted Vi's help. He'd known she was involved all along—and he hadn't told me.

It explained his hesitation last night when I asked him how he knew to take me and not Vi. It wasn't because I was more confident than she, or that we had a connection, it was because he'd met her.

"What is it, Hannah?" Langley asked.

"He lied to me," I muttered through my tears. I don't know when I'd begun to cry, but I couldn't stop myself. Vi and Jack had lied to me. People I thought I could trust. People I thought cared about me.

To make matters worse, I was a fire starter, and so much

about that was still shrouded in mystery. I needed to talk to someone about it, but there was no one I could completely trust. I'd never felt more alone in my life.

"Jack lies about a great many things." Langley signaled for Bollard to escort me to the door. "I thought you already knew that. I'm not sure why this has come as a surprise."

"I think I hate you," I said through my tears and clenched jaw.

"It'll pass, as will your feelings for Jack, both good and bad." He sighed and slouched over his papers. His voice when he spoke again sounded muffled, as if his mouth was buried in his collar. "Perhaps it's better for you both if you learn now just how much he has lied. The two of you together is a dangerous combination to yourselves and to others."

He was right, yet I hated hearing it.

"Good day, Hannah."

I ran past Bollard, down the corridor and outside. I wasn't dressed for walking, but I didn't care, nor did it matter. There was no need for coat or gloves, although sturdier shoes would have been nice. The heels may have been small but they weren't made for running and the soft leather was ruined by the time I reached the old abbey. The weak morning sun hadn't quite burned away all the mist and it hung over the lake like a cloud. The sky was a monotonous gray stretching endlessly above, and there wasn't a breath of wind in the air. Everything was so still, peaceful, the only sound came from my sobs, echoing around the ruins.

How many others had come to that place to cry? Had the Frakingham children before they were locked in the dungeon?

I leaned against the stones for support and buried my head in my hands. A thousand things raced through my mind, but one screamed louder than the rest.

What else had Jack lied about?

At some point I stopped crying, but I remained at the ruins. I couldn't face Sylvia and Langley yet, and something about the Abbey called to me. It had been a proud and majestic building once, dwarfing the landscape and reaching for the clouds. Monks had lived and worked there for hundreds of years, going about their daily ritual with purpose and a strong sense of themselves and their place in the world's order. But now it was just a collection of stones that barely resembled its original structure. It was broken and almost overrun by the higher power of Mother Nature. Much like me, if the fire inside me was indeed a natural thing I'd been born with. I truly had no idea.

I wandered through the ruins. The stones were cool and slippery, but that didn't stop me climbing some of the more stable walls. I inspected hidden nooks and pulled back the grass in places to see the foundations. After a while I knew the Abbey's layout and could picture the monks as they shuffled off to mass, or slept in their bare cells. It was a welcome activity and helped calm me, but my adventure was interrupted by the crunch of gravel on the long drive beneath Jack's horse's hooves. He didn't see me and rode straight up to the house. I thought about going after him, but decided against it. It didn't matter in the end. He came to me.

"I thought I might find you here." He stopped a few feet away and tapped his fingers thoughtfully on the flat top of a large stone. "You seem to like this place."

"At least I can't burn it. It's already ruined."

His Adam's apple bobbed erratically. "What happened is not your fault, Hannah. Don't blame yourself."

"I don't."

He nodded. "I've been to see August."

"There must be a reason you're telling me that."

Another nod. He took a few steps closer, but remained out of reach. He looked exhausted. His eyes were webbed with red lines and circled by dark shadows. Seeing him like that dissolved most of the lingering anger I felt toward him, but the sadness remained, a heavy weight pressing down on my chest. "He warned me that you were upset."

"You lied to me, Jack. I'd say I have good reason to be upset."

He leaned his hip against a low wall and regarded me. "You're right. I did lie. I wanted to protect you, but I suppose I should know by now that you don't need protecting. I'm sorry, Hannah."

"Tell me what role Violet played in my kidnap."

"I'm not entirely sure. I never spoke to her, only to your governess. She came to me in the grounds soon after my arrival and told me which girl to take. The short, freckly one, she said."

"*She* came to *you*?" I frowned. "So she already knew your purpose?"

He nodded and crossed his arms. "I don't know how. It may have been August's doing. But she gave me a time and place and true to her word, you were there."

"But what of Vi?"

He shrugged. "I assumed the governess enlisted her help to get you into the woods that day. I saw her in the cottage, you know."

"Before or after you kidnapped me?"

"After. I was about to carry you away when her face appeared at the window. She looked...odd. Sad, perhaps, or conflicted. I don't think her involvement was a decision she came to lightly, if that helps."

"I looked out for her every day of my life. I ensured Miss Levine never became cross with her, only with me. If she couldn't complete a task set by our tutors, I'd help her. If she was cold, I gave her my coat. Yet she abandoned me like I was nothing more to her than a doll she no longer wanted to play with. It doesn't matter how much she was involved. She just was."

I walked off and headed for the lake. Jack came up beside me, and I swiped away my tears. He shortened his stride to walk in time with my steps and he didn't take his gaze off me. Not that I was looking at him, but I could feel him watching me.

"I'm sorry I forced her to do it," he said. "And I'm sorry I didn't tell you. I thought it was best you didn't know. Can you forgive me?"

"I can if you don't lie to me again." I wanted him to talk to me about his past, about being Jack Cutler before he became Jack Langley, but he didn't. Until such time that he did, we could never be true friends, trusting one another implicitly.

It would seem I no longer had a single friend in the world. I turned my face to the lake, but didn't continue on. "Why would Vi betray me like that?" I asked. "Particularly if she were reluctant to do so."

"I can only guess."

"And what is your guess?"

"That she was given no choice, either by your governess or by Lord Wade himself."

"Lord Wade?" I chewed my lip. None of it made sense. Not Vi's involvement, not her father's and certainly not Langley's. I was still skeptical about his motives, even though I was now sure Jack and Sylvia weren't party to them. "How did Langley know where to find another fire starter?"

"He told me that Bollard had heard rumors in the village about a girl kept in an attic in a manor house who could set things on fire. He thinks the villagers must have heard it on the grapevine from the Windamere servants. It's not far from here. I'm sure some of the Harborough residents have been to the village near Windamere. You don't believe that?"

"I'm not sure. What troubles me is that it has happened *now*. Why?"

He shrugged. "The rumors may have been around for years, but Bollard has only just overheard them."

"Perhaps, but...don't you think it's odd that it coincided with the theft of your uncle's papers?"

"You think the two are linked?"

"I don't know, but it is strange that your friend was commissioned to perform the burglary right after I moved in, and that nothing of monetary value was stolen, only some of your uncle's papers. What was in those papers? How did the man who hired Patrick know where to look and what to look for? He gave Patrick some very specific instructions."

Jack pressed his lips together and put his hands on his hips. After a moment of staring at the lake, he spun round. "You're right. Too many questions." He strode off back to the house.

I picked up my skirts and ran to catch up with him. "Are you going to confront Langley?"

"Yes."

"Then I'm coming with you."

CHAPTER 12

"There you both are!" Sylvia said as Jack and I entered the house via the courtyard. "I've been looking for you. Were you in those horrible old ruins again?"

"I thought you liked the ruins," I said. "You've certainly painted them often enough."

"Only because there is little else to paint hereabouts. It's depressingly cold and damp in winter. I suppose that's why you like it."

"It does have a certain appeal," Jack said, absently. He seemed eager to get away, but I could see that she needed to talk about something.

"Is everything all right?" I asked.

"Yes. No. That is, I wanted to apologize to you, Hannah."

"Me? Why?"

"Because when it was revealed that you weren't Lady Violet, my reaction may have made it seem as if I were..."

"Disgusted?" Jack offered, crossing his arms and lifting one eyebrow.

"I was shocked," she said. "Why are you smirking at me like that, Jack? This is between Hannah and me."

"Anything that concerns Hannah also concerns me." He

leaned down so that he was nose to nose with her. "And I just wanted to see how you'd get out of this with your polite façade intact. I seem to recall you having a similar reaction when August took me in. You never apologized to me for being...shocked."

"Then you recall incorrectly." She sniffed. When he smiled, she shoved his shoulder. "Go away. Haven't you got better things to do than torment me?"

"As a matter of fact, we do."

"We're going to speak to your uncle and get some answers." I grasped her hand and gave it a squeeze. I wanted her to know I appreciated her seeking me out to apologize. It meant more than she would ever know. "Would you like to come?"

"Not particularly," she said. But when Jack and I walked off, she followed.

Jack went to barge past Bollard as he opened his uncle's door. The servant put out his arm to stop him, but Jack simply squared up to him, smiled, and politely said, "Move, or I'll set your shirt on fire."

"Let them in," Langley said with a frustrated sigh. "What is it, Jack? I thought we already discussed the rebuilding arrangements."

"Is that where you went this morning?" Sylvia asked.

Jack nodded. "I've contracted a builder from the village. He's going to work off the original plans for Frakingham and replicate the destroyed section."

She pulled a face. "Perhaps he could make it a little less Gothic. Arches and gloom are out of fashion."

"That's not why we're here," Jack said to Langley. "We need to talk about what Patrick said."

Langley must have had a spare wheelchair stored somewhere because he sat in another, smaller one, the first no doubt having been reduced to ashes. He had wheeled around to face us when we entered, but now he turned away. "It's none of your business."

"It bloody well is!" Jack grasped the handles of the chair

and pulled it around so that his uncle faced him. Langley's nostrils flared, but his gaze didn't flicker as he glared back at his nephew. "Who is the one-armed man?" Jack ground out. "Who hired Patrick to burgle you?"

"It's all in hand—"

"Tell us!"

Langley folded his hands in his lap. "I appreciate your concern for me—"

"I don't want to pursue this for *you*." Jack straightened and closed his fists at his sides, but not before I saw the glow of his fingers. He was furious, but controlling it. Barely. "I want to get to the bottom of this for Hannah's sake. The theft may have something to do with her abduction."

"What makes you think that?"

"The timing is too coincidental for the events not to be linked. Since you orchestrated her kidnap, and I suspect you know who the one-armed gentleman is, you must know why there's a connection."

"Jack," Langley said on another sigh. The wrinkles around his eyes folded in on each other and his shoulders slumped forward. "The man is dangerous and shouldn't be trifled with. I contacted the constabulary after I realized who it was from Bollard's account. Let the detective inspector do his job."

"The inspector is incompetent. He didn't question all of the staff after the burglary."

"He has the man's name. All he needs to do is arrest him." He lifted a hand and waved Jack away. "Leave me. I have work to do."

Jack muttered something under his breath then stormed out. Sylvia, chewing her lip, followed him. I remained behind despite Bollard looming beside me.

"For an intelligent man, that was a very stupid thing to do," I said.

"You're still here?" Langley said without turning around from his work.

"Jack is far more capable than the constabulary. If you

want this man punished, you should give Jack some information."

"Are you quite finished?"

"Now you've riled him, which is something you seem to like doing to the people who live with you."

"Hannah," he said, finally looking at me over his shoulder, "Jack has a job to do here. Training you. He can't go gallivanting around the country."

"Then perhaps he needs a new job."

***

Jack and I trained in the bare room for the rest of the day, and the next. He was edgy and frustrated, and it was difficult for us both to concentrate. I made painfully little progress in learning to willfully produce the fire within me, and therefore absolutely none in dampening it. It wasn't surprising since it required me to be angry, something I couldn't simply turn on at will. The eventual aim, Jack said, was that I would be able to set things alight with a mere thought, and quell the heat at times when my temper got the better of me.

On the morning of what would have been the third straight day of training, Tommy gave us some startling news over breakfast. Or, I should say, he gave Jack the news. The two of them exchanged whispers in the corner before Tommy took up his position near the sideboard.

"Bloody hell," Jack muttered, thumping the solid surface of the sideboard with his fist.

"What is it?" I asked.

"There was another break-in last night. Tommy scared the man away. He and Olson kept watch for the rest of the night. You should have woken me," he said to the footman.

"Yes, sir."

"Stop with the sirs when it's just us, will you? You know I hate it."

Tommy's usually dour expression lifted. "Yes, sir."

Jack gave him a withering glare, and Sylvia covered her giggle with her hand.

"Was anything taken?" I asked.

"No."

"Was it Patrick?"

"No, Miss Smith," Tommy said. "It wasn't anyone I recognized."

"Dear lord," Sylvia said, sitting heavily on a chair. "What if he intended to murder us in our beds?"

"I'm sure that wasn't his intention, Syl," Jack said.

Tommy puffed out his chest. "I'll protect you, Miss Langley."

"Thank you," she said. "I can rely on you if not my own cousin."

"Have the police been notified?" I asked.

"Yes, Miss Smith," said Tommy.

Indeed, the inspector and constable appeared just before luncheon. It was the same ones who'd come the first time, and I was surprised to see them. Weren't they supposed to be arresting the one-armed man? I was dying to find out more, although I doubted Langley would tell me anything. Jack and I watched the policemen leave from the window, our lessons having been abandoned early because neither of us could concentrate or stop speculating about the intruder.

"I hope they spoke to everyone this time," I said as the policemen climbed into their carriage.

"I'm more interested in what they said to August about the one-armed man. And what he said to them. Come on, let's find out."

We went straight to Langley's room where we found him reading in bed. Neither Bollard nor the wheelchair were in sight. The room was much smaller than the previous one in the burnt out eastern wing, and there was little space for anything other than the bed, a writing desk, a wardrobe and a few chairs. Langley had filled up much of the remaining floor space since our last visit. Singed papers piled up near the desk, and broken or burned pieces of equipment filled boxes and crates. Microscopes, tools and jars that had escaped the fire covered the relatively small surface of his desk.

"I suppose you wish to resume your questioning," Langley said without looking up from his book.

"You suppose correctly," Jack said. "We saw the police leave. What did the inspector have to say? Have they arrested the one-armed man?"

Langley closed the book and set it down on the bedside table. "They couldn't arrest him."

Jack went very still. "Why not?"

"He claimed not to know anyone named Patrick in London. He said the thief must have lied to you to protect himself. He said he has no interest in my papers."

"And they believed him?"

"You have no idea how convincing he can be."

"Do *you* believe him?" I asked.

"No. But look at it from the inspector's perspective. He cannot arrest a gentleman based on the word of a criminal. Not without other evidence."

"What a farce," Jack muttered.

"What are we to do?" I asked. "He cannot be allowed to get away with it."

Jack nodded. "Patrick's life is in danger, and by extension the lives of the charges he cares for."

"Charges?"

"He takes care of orphans using money I send him."

"My money," Langley said.

Were the children linked to Jack's past? I suspected they were, but I wanted him to tell me of his own accord, not because I peppered him with questions, but because he wanted to.

"Let me confront the one-armed man," Jack said.

"No," Langley said. "What good will that do?"

"If I can get him to admit it, I'll be another witness."

"And when it's discovered that you know Patrick? No jury would convict him."

"What if he admits it in front of witnesses?" Jack said. "Or the police?"

Langley picked up his book and flipped it open to a page near the middle. I could have sworn when he first set it down he was at the beginning. "You're not going," he said.

Jack stepped up to the bed, but there was nothing threatening about his stance. He did ooze a kind of self-assuredness and power, however. "I'm twenty-two, August. I have able legs and a voice. Let me use them."

Langley stared down at the book in his lap. The knuckles holding it were white, the thumbs digging into the pages.

"I can find out who this man is without you telling me," Jack went on. "There can't be too many gentlemen matching the description Patrick gave. So why not just make it easier and tell me."

Langley closed his eyes.

"With or without your help, August. You have a choice."

Langley's eyes opened. I was surprised to see worry in their depths. "It doesn't sound like it." When Jack didn't answer, he added, "I could hire someone privately. I've done it before."

"To do what?"

"To find people."

Did he mean me? Jack?

"I see." Jack stood again. "I had no idea. I thought Bollard was your only lackey."

"I can't always spare Bollard. I am a businessman, Jack, and businessmen hire people from time to time."

"And here I thought you were a mad scientist," I said.

Langley's lips stretched into a strained smile. "Very amusing."

"I am involved whether you like it or not," Jack said. "If you wanted to hire someone to confront this man, then I suspect you would have done it instead of sending those incompetent policemen."

"I'd hoped to solve this in a legal manner."

"We still can. I want to confront him."

"He's dangerous."

Jack seemed to notice what he'd said at the same time I

did. Or rather, what he didn't say. He didn't say 'no.'

"Give me a name, August. Trust me for once."

"I do trust you."

"Then prove it."

Someone cleared his throat behind us, and we all turned. Bollard stood in the open doorway, his unreadable gaze on his master. The small sound was so peculiar coming from the usually silent servant that I gasped.

"Very well, Jack," Langley said. "I'll tell you everything you need to know about Reuben Tate. You'd better sit down. Both of you."

I sat in the armchair near the window and Jack pulled a separate hardback chair closer to the bed. Bollard shut the door and came to stand beside the bed like an obedient dog.

"Reuben Tate and I were partners," Langley said.

"Partners in what?" I asked.

"Don't interrupt. We owned a laboratory together and shared research. It seemed the sensible, economical thing to do since we were both in need of funds and our research interests were the same. It was our joint efforts that led to the development of a drug."

"A drug to cure what?"

"That is not your concern, Hannah. Reuben and I had a falling out over it. I wanted to sell the remedy to a large company with the facilities to manufacture it on a grand scale, but Reuben wanted to borrow money to expand our laboratory and produce it there. I won."

"I'm sure you did," I muttered.

"We both benefitted financially from the sale. I bought this house and investments then sold off my portion of the laboratory to Tate. We parted ways after that and haven't seen each other since."

"So why is he stealing your papers?" Jack asked.

"I can only guess that he's in financial straits again and needs a new cure to sell." He waved his hand, as is if his one-time friend's difficulties were no longer of concern to him.

"He stole your research?" I asked.

"Some of it. I had Bollard bury the important formulas that weren't taken during the first burglary."

So that's what he was doing in the woods the day I tried to escape!

"Reuben always did have a gambling problem," Langley said. "I suspect his debts have piled up again."

"But didn't you sell the other drug for a fortune?" I asked. "If your half bought this house, he must have gotten a sizeable amount too."

"I received more than half since I'd invested most of the funds in the first place. We had an agreement drawn up to reflect the proportions early on." He thrust out his chin. "It was another thing Reuben resented."

"Did he resent anything more?"

"The fact that I'm a better microbiologist than he is."

"And you think that's why he's thieving now? Money difficulties?" Jack asked.

"Perhaps. Whatever his reasons, I doubt it has anything to do with Hannah's escape from Windamere."

He was calling it an escape now, was he? It still felt like an abduction to me, but I let the comment pass.

"It's purely a coincidence," Langley said. "It must be." When neither Jack nor I spoke, he added, "Knowing Reuben, his debts have become unmanageable and he is desperate for money. Selling a new drug, *my* drug, will alleviate the pressure."

"If you haven't seen him for some years," Jack said, "how would he know you were working on a remedy?"

"Because he knows me very well, and I'm always working on something."

Langley dictated the address of Reuben Tate's laboratory to Bollard who wrote it down and gave the piece of paper to Jack.

"Hackney Wick," I said, reading it. "Is that far from here? I confess, I've not heard of it."

Langley grunted. "I'm sure there are many places you've never heard of, Hannah. It's not your fault."

"I may not have been to many places, Mr. Langley, but I can assure you I was given access to maps and books. I know where most villages in England are."

Indeed, I had often spread out maps on the floor of our parlor and studied every detail. I'd imagine what each village looked like, what the people did there. When he could, my geography tutor provided books about the places that described the landscape and history of a particular area, and I would study them as if I were leading an expedition. It was silly now that I think about it, but I would imagine myself as an explorer finding undiscovered lands. Every piece of England was like a foreign country to me, having seen nothing further than the Windamere estate boundary, but in truth, there probably wasn't much of the exotic about Derbyshire or Hampshire, Cornwall or Yorkshire.

"Hackney Wick isn't a village," Jack said. "It's part of London, albeit on the edge." He pocketed the paper. "I'll head off today."

"So soon?" I said. "But you won't get there before nightfall."

"I'll spend a night in an inn along the way. Don't worry. I can take care of myself." He was looking at me when he started the sentence, but by the end, he'd turned to Langley.

Langley picked up his book and began to read. "I'll see you in a few days."

***

Jack left in the carriage with Olsen driving. I found it difficult to settle to any task, but considering most of the tasks available to me involved needlework, it wasn't surprising. When I couldn't focus on a sensation novel that I'd borrowed from Sylvia, I decided it was time to get out of the house. I suggested a walk, but she had other ideas.

"We could go into the village," she said. "Mrs. Moore said the smoky smell won't come out of some of our clothes. I'm sure Uncle will give us money for new garments."

"He's probably in need of some himself. Most of his personal belongings would have been destroyed."

"Bollard has already been into the village on his behalf."

"He's very devoted to your uncle."

"Very."

"Do you know how long they've known each other?"

"A very long time." She pulled a face. "Let's not talk about Bollard. He's so dreary." She put her embroidery back in her sewing basket and grasped my hand. "Let's go this minute."

"But Jack has the carriage and Olsen."

"Tommy will drive us in the brougham. It's smaller than the clarence, but it'll suffice for the short journey."

We sent Tommy to give word to Langley that we were going shopping in Harborough then asked him to prepare the brougham, Langley's second carriage. Fifteen minutes later, we were about to climb into the cabin when a rickety farmer's cart pulled by an old nag lumbered up the drive.

"Who could that be?" Sylvia asked, squinting into the sunlight.

Tommy greeted the farmer and patted the horse's nose as two young lads hopped off the back of the cart. "Bloody hell!" Tommy said. "What are you doing here?"

One of the lads dropped a coin into the farmer's palm. The farmer nodded at Sylvia and me, then turned his nag around and plodded off the way he'd come.

The two newcomers looked up at Frakingham, holding their caps to their heads as they leaned backward to take it all in. They were a grimy couple. Dirt seemed to have set up residence in the creases of their hands and faces, and their filthy clothes were covered in patches. The taller lad's toes stuck out of the end of his boots and his sleeves reached halfway up his arms. The shorter boy sniffed incessantly. I recognized him as the one who'd peered out of the window of the house where Jack had met Patrick in London. Whatever was he doing here? Where was Patrick?

Oh no. Dear lord no. Horror twisted my gut, and I was glad when Sylvia hooked her arm through mine. I clasped her tightly and shushed her with a raise of my finger when she began to speak.

Tommy bent down to the sniffly lad's level. "What's happened?" he asked.

"'E's dead," said the boy, his bottom lip wobbling.

My stomach dove. I gripped Sylvia tighter and she sidled closer. Tommy swore, a sure sign that he was deeply affected. He took his footman duties very seriously, and swearing in the presence of Sylvia and me was a serious offense in his own mind, if not in mine.

"Paddy knew somefing was going to 'appen to 'im," the lad said. "That night Jack came, Paddy told us to come to Freak 'Ouse if the worst 'appened. 'E told us 'ow to get 'ere and gave us money for the journey. 'E said you'd take care o' us, Tommy. You and Jack."

"Of course we will," Tommy said. "You'll be safe here. But what about the others?"

"They're still in Plum Alley."

"Who's taking care of them?"

"Huh?"

"Is there someone in charge now that Patrick is gone?"

"No," the taller lad said. "We got no one else."

"What about Miss Charity?"

"No one's seen 'er for months."

Tommy shook his head. "Do the children have enough food for a few days?"

Silence as the two boys looked down at their boots.

"Why not? Jack sent money to Patrick regularly. He was supposed to use it to care for you all."

"'E did," said Sniffles.

"'E didn't," the other boy protested. "'E bought the worst food, the stuff that's gone rotted. Sometimes it stank like old feet, or it 'ad somefing crawling in it."

Tommy clicked his tongue. "And I can see from your clothing that he didn't buy you anything new or warm like Jack instructed."

"Paddy bought 'imself good clobber," the second lad said. "For 'is woman too."

Tommy swore then apologized to Sylvia and me.

"How did Patrick die?" I asked the boys.

Sniffles wiped his nose with his sleeve. "We woke up two days ago and 'e was lying on the ground. Blood everywhere."

"Smashed 'is 'ead in, they did," the other lad said. "Right mess, it were." He spoke with more detachment than Sniffles, as if he took such violence for granted.

"Oh, my," Sylvia whispered, turning her face away.

"Right then, lads," Tommy said, standing. "You'll be taken care of here and we'll see to the welfare of the others. Come with me and we'll speak to Mrs. Moore. She'll find you somewhere to sleep and maybe some clean clothes. You can stay until Jack gets back, but not forever." He glared at the house as he said it, as if he knew it was futile to ask Langley.

"Should we go to the others in London?" Sylvia asked me as Tommy walked off with the boys. "Something must be done to help them, or they'll end up thieving. Jack and Tommy would be terribly upset if one of them were caught. They'd be jailed for certain."

I nodded absently. I was concerned for the children, but there was something more pressing to consider. "Patrick must have been murdered by Reuben Tate," I said. "And Jack has gone to see him."

Sylvia gasped. "You truly think Tate did it?"

"I think it likely. Patrick was afraid to tell Jack who paid him to steal the papers. He said his life would be in danger if he did. I don't think Jack quite believed him."

"Then Jack doesn't know how dangerous Tate is. Oh dear lord."

"We have to warn him, Sylvia. We have to leave today. Right now."

CHAPTER 13

"Do you think your uncle will allow us to go?" I asked Sylvia. We'd remained near the carriage, trying to decide whether to obtain Langley's permission to follow Jack or not. It boiled down to this single question, and her answer.

She pulled up the collar of her coat and sunk her chin into the fur. "No."

"That's settled then. We'll go anyway."

"Hannah! That's terribly rebellious of you."

"Rebellion would be leaving and not returning." I clasped her arm. "We can't let Jack stroll into a meeting with Tate without being completely aware of the danger."

"He has his fire to protect him."

"What if Tate has a gun? Or drugs him?"

"Yes, of course you're right."

"If we hurry, we'll catch him on the road or at least arrive soon after."

"Uncle could send somebody else," she said. "Tommy or Bollard."

"We'll take Tommy anyway." She still hesitated, so I added, "I've been kept in an attic most of my life, only doing what I've been told to do by others, going where I'm told to go. If coming here has taught me anything, it's that I am a free person now. I make my own decisions."

"I don't know," she hedged. "Uncle will be very angry, and I'm dependent on him. We both are."

"He won't throw us out. Not when he went to so much trouble to get me."

"Precisely: to get *you*. Not *me*." Tears filled her eyes and she blinked rapidly. "I am nobody."

"You're his niece!" I didn't feel quite as certain as I sounded. In many ways, she was as much a prisoner at Frakingham as I had been at Windamere. Most women were in one way or another. We weren't allowed to own property or open bank accounts, and many professions and educational institutions were closed to us. Now that I had left the only home I'd ever known, I was beginning to realize how much my welfare was in the hands of others.

"You're braver than I," she said.

"It doesn't feel like it. My heart is trying to break through my ribs. I'm determined to ignore it. For Jack." And for me. I needed to do this to assure myself I wasn't Langley's prisoner, that I could get away if I wanted to. I wouldn't allow myself to be locked up again.

"I'll get Tommy," I said before she could protest again.

When Tommy and I returned to the carriage, we found Sylvia waiting. She didn't look any less concerned, but at least she was still there.

"Let's go immediately." She extended her hand for Tommy to help her up the step. "We have coats and money. Uncle will still think we're going shopping in Harborough, but we'll go on to Hackney Wick instead."

"Excellent." I smiled at her. "You're turning out to be quite the rebel yourself, Sylvia."

"I want to go shopping in London after this is all over. Since we're not taking a change of clothes, we'll have to visit Oxford Street again."

At least she'd agreed to come.

***

We didn't find Jack on the road. He must have traveled

faster than us, which wasn't surprising since he had the better carriage and horses to pull it. We stayed overnight at an inn on the way, and reached Hackney Wick late in the morning.

The suburb was indeed at the edge of the great city and we came upon it suddenly. The open spaces of the countryside gave way to featureless, interchangeable terraced houses and brick factories that spewed smoke from dozens of chimneys. Their high walls blocked passersby from seeing the machinations behind. Not that there were many passersby. I could count the number who walked the muddy street on one hand. Who could blame people for staying indoors? The air stank and the machinery beyond the walls whirred and clanged in an endless drone. We kept the window closed.

The carriage slowed in front of a double-story building squashed between two large factories like a small child smothered by fat adults. It was built of brown brick like everything else on the street, but it was a house, not a factory. The brickwork above the two top-most windows was blackened up to the roofline.

"Do you think this is it?" Sylvia asked. "Do you think he lives there too?"

"Langley didn't say. I do know it houses Tate's laboratory and factory. I can see the chimney stacks of the factory behind."

"There's no smoke."

Indeed there wasn't. The factory mustn't have been in operation. That would align with Langley's theory that Tate needed money quickly and by nefarious means. If his factory wasn't operational, he likely had no income.

Tommy opened the door for us and we stepped down to the unpaved road. "I'll lead the way," he said.

"Don't be absurd," Sylvia scolded. "You're a footman. You may escort us inside, but remain a little behind. I don't particularly want to meet this man on our own."

I didn't think Tommy's presence would make any

difference to Tate. As Sylvia so bluntly put it, Tommy was a footman and few gentlemen paid attention to servants. To people of Langley, Wade and Tate's ilk, footmen were as featureless and interchangeable as the Hackney Wick houses.

"Do you think Jack is here?" Tommy asked, looking up and down the street. "I don't see Olsen or the carriage anywhere."

"He may have sent him away," Sylvia said.

"Why would he do that?"

Why indeed. The unease that had been lurking beneath the surface since leaving Frakingham made itself known in the most intense way. Fear drilled into my core. One man was dead. *Please God, don't let Jack be next.*

"I don't think you should come with us," I said to Tommy.

"What?" Sylvia cried. "Why not?"

"Tate doesn't know that we know about Patrick. Bringing Tommy may alert him to the fact he's here for our protection. Besides, while we're distracting Tate, Tommy can get into the factory and look around."

"That's very devious," she said. I wasn't sure if it was a compliment or not.

"What about the brougham?" Tommy asked.

"We passed some stables around the corner near the fire engine-station. Take it there and walk back. If Tate is watching us, then he'll think you've left. There must be another entrance into the factory that doesn't go through the front house. See if you can find it."

Tommy grinned. "It's a good plan, Miss Smith."

"And dangerous," Sylvia said.

"Thank you for your concern for my safety, Miss Langley, I'll be alright."

She sniffed. "I meant it would be dangerous for us alone."

"Oh. Right." Tommy tipped his cap then hopped up to the driver's seat. "I'll meet you back at the stables." He flicked the reins and drove off.

"I don't like this," Sylvia said, watching him go. "I don't like this at all."

"You have to stop worrying. It's written all over your face. Never let the enemy see your fear."

"Where did you learn that little gem of wisdom? A book on battle techniques?"

"As a matter of fact, yes. Come on."

I walked off and when Sylvia caught up to me, I was glad to see she didn't look as if she wanted to throw up her breakfast anymore. "Do you suppose Jack has already been here and left?" she asked.

"It's entirely likely. He may have even gone to fetch the police, or be on his way back to Frakingham already. But we're here now and we must go inside and find out for sure. Just in case..." I couldn't say it, couldn't hear the words out loud.

"Yes," Sylvia said heavily. "Just in case."

A housekeeper wearing a spotless white apron answered the door upon our knock. I took this as a good sign. The presence of such a matronly looking woman was a comfort. Tate wouldn't do anything with her near, surely.

She directed us to sit in the small downstairs parlor while she fetched her employer. We hadn't been waiting one minute when the man I assumed to be Reuben Tate walked in.

He wasn't very tall, but he was whip-thin and hollow-cheeked. He was about Langley's age if the white hair was an indication, but where Langley had wrinkles around his eyes and across his forehead, Tate had none. His face was as smooth as a polished tabletop, and just as shiny. Indeed, the hair at his ears was slightly damp too. The shirt sleeve that should have housed a left arm was folded and pinned to the side of his waistcoat. He wore no smoking jacket or house coat, but he didn't look like the sort who went for such a casual appearance anyway. He was too neatly dressed. His hair was perfectly combed and his chin cleanly shaved. Much like his face, there wasn't a single wrinkle in his clothes and the shirt collar and trouser creases were sharp.

"Welcome," he said, giving us a shallow bow. "I commend you both on your courage. I could see that it wasn't an easy decision to send your driver away and speak to me by yourselves."

So he had indeed been watching us. I was glad that I'd guessed correctly and sent Tommy on his own errand, but disturbed too. I was also deeply disturbed that Jack wasn't there, yet not particularly surprised. When we'd not seen the carriage outside, I knew we'd missed him. Clearly he hadn't managed to get Tate arrested.

Sylvia shifted uneasily beside me. "My name is Sylvia Langley," she said, thrusting out her chin. "I believe you know my uncle."

"How is August?" Tate asked. He didn't seem surprised to hear her name, and I wondered if he'd recognized her somehow, or expected her.

The polite response seemed to catch her unawares. "H, he's w, well, thank you."

"Good. I'm glad to hear it. And who is your charming companion?" He turned a rather bland smile onto me, but behind it was genuine curiosity.

"My name is Hannah Smith," I said. "I'm a friend of the Langleys."

His sharp intake of breath preceded a long pause in which he studied my face, my hair. I felt a blush rise to my skin and I looked down, away. In less time than it took to blink, he was crouching before me. He touched his long finger to my chin and made me look at him, so he could finish his study. I jerked away, and he slowly backed up to his seat without taking his gaze off me.

"Hannah," he murmured. "Hannah...Smith. Of course. Of *course.*" He chuckled to himself and thumped the chair arm with his palm.

I glanced at Sylvia and she lifted one shoulder. She had no idea what Tate was talking about either. One moment he was a civil gentleman, and the next he was mumbling to himself and cackling like a witch. It seemed August Langley wasn't the only mad scientist in England.

"You haven't been under August's roof this entire time," he said. "I would have noticed."

"No. I haven't."

"Mr. Tate," Sylvia said in a crisp tone that was reminiscent of Miss Levine. "We're looking for my cousin, Jack Langley. Has he been here?"

Tate either ignored her or didn't hear. He was once more looking at me with such earnest that I wanted the chair to swallow me up. It was as if I'd delivered a miraculous cure to a dying man or offered up a profound piece of wisdom. I wasn't afraid of him, but I was unnerved and very curious. How did he know my name? How did Langley? Tate might hold some answers to key questions that Langley wouldn't give up.

"Do you know me?" I asked, breathless.

"Yes. And no." He grinned, revealing crooked, yellow teeth. They were at odds with his neat, crisp clothing. "Hannah Smith, where have you been for the last eighteen years? I've been looking for you."

"How do you know who I am?"

"Hannah," Sylvia said, "perhaps we shouldn't be asking Mr. Tate that sort of question without Uncle present."

"Don't listen to her," Tate said. His top lip pared back in a sneer. "Langley doesn't have your best interests at heart, Miss Smith. I know him far better than both of you, and I know he cares nothing for you."

"I beg your pardon," Sylvia said huffily. "You know nothing of the sort."

The housekeeper re-entered carrying a tray. She poured tea for us then left without a glance back. Once she was gone, Sylvia grabbed my hand. "We're going. Clearly Jack isn't here."

I patted her hand and she caught it too, trapping both of mine. "I want to hear what he has to say," I said.

"Please, Hannah," she whispered. "Let's go."

Tate handed a cup and saucer to Sylvia. "At least stay for tea. You might also find what I have to say interesting."

"I *want* to stay," I said to her. "Just for a few minutes."

Her fingers tightened around my hands, then she let go. She accepted the cup then put it down on the table. "No. Come, Hannah."

I shook my head. Tate pressed the very edge of his lips to the rim of his cup and sipped. "I'm not the enemy, Miss Langley. I've made some mistakes in the past, but I'm not out to harm either of you, whatever Langley has led you to believe."

"He hasn't led us to believe anything," Sylvia muttered.

"What has he told you about me?"

"That you two were partners once," I said, "and that you bought his share of the business with your proceeds from the sale of a drug."

He took another sip. "The bare facts. True enough in essence."

"Mr. Tate," said Sylvia, "where is my cousin?"

A small crease connected his eyebrows and, after his gaze flicked to the door, it finally settled on her. He took another sip and regarded Sylvia over the rim of the cup. "Don't fret, Miss Langley, he's well. After we talked he wanted to explore the factory. My assistant has taken him on a tour."

Out of the corner of my eye, I saw Sylvia turn to me. I didn't need to see her face to know she was confounded by Tate's calm manner. I was too. I almost preferred the slightly hysterical chuckling. This blank evenness felt unnatural. He was hiding something, and by the way the teacup trembled, it had to be either excitement or fear. Considering we were young, female and in his home, I doubted it was the latter.

"Why would he want a tour?" I asked. "Jack came here to confront you over the theft of Mr. Langley's papers. Do you deny you stole them?"

"No."

"So you admit it!" Sylvia scowled. "Then why hasn't Jack had you arrested?"

"Because we had a very profound discussion, and he no longer believed involving the police was necessary. Shall I tell you what I told him?"

I desperately wanted to say yes. I suspected the things he'd said to Jack were tightly interwoven with my own burning questions about how Tate and Langley knew me. But Sylvia was right. We needed to ensure Jack was safe first. Afterward, I would seek out the answers.

"We'd like to see him," I said.

"Let him be, ladies. A lad like Jack needs time away from women and prattle once in a while. There can't be much for him at Frakingham with only you two and that cripple for company."

The one-armed man was calling the wheelchair-bound man a cripple? If my sense of humor hadn't been leached out of me by Tate's odd declarations, I would have laughed out loud.

"Our conversations are quite lively, thank you very much," Sylvia said with a sniff.

Tate pulled a handkerchief from the pocket of his waistcoat and dabbed his forehead, but the shine remained. "Tell me, Miss Langley, does your uncle still have that silent ogre hovering about? I remember when he first came to work for August."

"Bollard? Yes, why?"

His lips flattened and he carefully re-folded his handkerchief on his knee. "He's not what he seems, you know. He's...devious. Watch him, Miss Langley. Watch him very closely. That's my advice to you."

I was beginning to think Tate would win if there were a Mad Scientist competition between him and Langley. No wonder they'd fallen out. Two such men in a confined space would be a formula for an explosive relationship.

"We'd like to see Jack," I demanded. "Immediately."

His lips flattened. "As you wish. But first, let me tell you what I told him. I'd like the chance to defend myself. What I'm about to tell you not only eased Jack's mind, it spurred his interest in what I'm doing here. Shall we talk as we walk to the factory?"

"I don't know," Sylvia said, chewing her lip.

"I'll also tell you how I know you, Miss Smith." He smiled at me in a way that could only be described as sweet. I was no longer sure how to take Tate. My instincts were confused. One moment he was all kindness, the next he was being odd and evasive. So I set instinct aside and used my head. I wanted answers, and if I needed to follow him to get them, I would. If there was a chance that Jack was there, we had to find out for sure.

"We'll come," I said, standing. Sylvia seemed relieved to have the decision made for her.

Tate rose and indicated we should walk ahead. "I'd better begin at the beginning. No doubt August told you that he and I fell out over money, and that I stole his papers so that I could reproduce his latest remedy and sell it. He always did pretend I was the greedy one, when in truth it was he all along."

"What do you mean?" I asked. We walked slowly out of the parlor and back into the entrance hall. An Oriental rug deadened the sound of our shoes on the tiles. It was a new rug, the pile still thick, and it ran the length of the narrow hall. Another rug covered the stairs, and it too looked new, as did the hat stand, table and framed mirror. The faint smell of paint hung in the air, but I could see no artworks. The walls must have been freshly painted.

"He has always wanted that which his betters had," Tate went on. "A grand house, horses, carriages, land. To him, those things meant status and respect, two things he desired more than any...well, more than the use of his legs." He paused at the front door. "You know this to be true, don't you, Miss Langley?"

Sylvia looked down at her feet. Her nod was slight, but noticeable.

"Your uncle was the one who wanted to sell the remedy for the most money we could get. I didn't want to sell it at all."

"I don't like you besmirching my uncle's name," Sylvia said.

"Then block your ears."

"What was the remedy for?" I asked.

"To combat an insidious disease," he said. "You wouldn't have heard of it."

I was beginning to get the feeling there was more to their remedy than they were telling us.

Tate held the door open, and we walked outside once again. The small front garden had little to recommend it. It was sparse and winter-bare, with only a few low-growing herbs planted in square beds, and several dormant roses spaced precisely apart along the fence. A stone path led to the side of the house and we followed it. "Your uncle may have wanted the money, but I wanted the glory of the discovery. See, we each have our weaknesses, Miss Langley, but I'm not afraid to reveal mine. I wanted to sell the rights to manufacture the drug to another company better equipped to do it, but keep control over its dissemination and packaging. August didn't care about that since few companies with deep pockets weren't interested in a deal that didn't give them total control. He won, of course. He usually did when we disagreed. I think you both know how...immovable he can be."

"So why did you steal his research?" I asked as we slowly made our way down the side of the house. It was damp and dark beneath the shadows of the house on one side and the wall of the neighboring factory on the other. "Do you want to pass off his new drug as your own?"

"No. This time it's different. I'll admit that I have debts. I like to spend money and...unforeseen circumstances have meant a large outlay recently. But that's not why I took his papers which, I might add, didn't have everything I needed to replicate the remedy."

"Good," said Sylvia.

"Long before August and I developed the remedy that

made us rich, we were working on another experiment."

"What has this to do with anything?" she asked.

Tate paused and looked at me, but I already knew. It had to do with me. "August and I belonged to a group called the Society For Supernatural Activity. It's not exactly a secret organization, but they're not very open about what they do. I won't go into the details, but suffice it to say the members like to dabble in the supernatural."

Sylvia snorted. "What rot. There's no such thing as ghosts and what not." She flapped her hand, but neither Tate nor I paid her much attention. Weren't Jack and I proof that supernatural phenomena did exist?

"Why do the members like to dabble, Mr. Tate?" I asked.

"To see if it exists or not."

"I'm surprised that it interests you. Doesn't believing in such things go against everything scientists stand for?"

"For many, yes. Not for August and me. We wanted to study these phenomena, to see how they work and try to replicate them in a laboratory environment. We thought if we could identify what caused paranormal traits in humans, we might be able to harness it."

"And sell it."

"Yes."

I stopped and put a hand to the wall of the house. The moss-covered bricks cooled my palm, but I had difficulty catching my breath. It felt like a weight was pressing down on my chest, pushing the air out of me. "What am I, Mr. Tate?"

"You are a rare fire starter," he said softly. In the dim light of the shadowy path, it was difficult to see him clearly, but his eyes sparkled with tears. "But you already knew that."

"Yes. Jack and I are the only ones."

He shook his head. "No, you're not. There's another."

"Who?"

We'd reached the factory door, and he held it open for us. The door sported thick bolts, but none were locked. The heavy wood seemed new, the paint fresh. The bricks of the small factory were blackened above the doorway and the single boarded-up window to the right. Same as the house. There were no other windows on the one-story building that I could see. No sign of Jack, either, or indeed anyone else. I spared a thought for Tommy and hoped he had not yet arrived.

"I'll tell you inside," Tate said. "Jack's in there, and he's very curious about the same things as you, Miss Smith. I'll tell you together."

"Everything?" I asked.

"Yes. The entire story, dating back almost twenty-two years."

"Wait!" Sylvia gripped my arm and pulled me back along the path, out of earshot. Tate didn't come after us, but kept on smiling. "It might be a trick," she hissed into my ear.

"There's a very good chance that it is," I said gravely.

"Then we have to leave!"

"No. Jack might be in there and in difficulty."

"I doubt it. Jack doesn't get himself into difficulties, only out of them. He at least can set things on fire at will. You can't."

"I can if I'm angry, and I can assure you I'll be furious if Tate is lying. Sylvia, I have to find out what he knows. Do you understand how important this is to me? He has the answers to questions I've longed to know, not only about my fire starting, but about my parents. Finding those answers means...everything." My throat squeezed shut with the effort not to cry. I hadn't meant to sound so vehement, nor had I expected to want answers so badly that I would walk into a suspected trap. But I did. God, how I wanted to learn what Tate knew. I suddenly felt like half a person, with a major part of my life missing. Tate could fill in the hollow spaces.

I had to know and I would do anything to get those answers. Anything.

I walked away from her and back to Tate. As I stepped through the doorway, the faint odor of damp ashes filled my nostrils. I could only see what lay within the beam of natural light, yet even that disappeared when Tate shut the door on Sylvia, himself and me.

But not before I saw the twisted and blackened metal of broken machines, the burnt beams and tools, and the utter devastation wrought by fire.

"Is there a lamp, Mr. Tate?" Sylvia tried her best to sound commanding, but the wobble in her voice was unmistakable. "Light it this instant!"

I headed toward her voice and found her outstretched hands, searching for me. She latched onto me and we clasped each other. Her heartbeat hammered against my shoulder, her limbs trembled. She was terrified, and that would make her useless. It was up to me. I had to keep the fear at bay otherwise the anger wouldn't come.

"Where's Jack?" I demanded.

"I thought you wanted answers. Don't you want to know who the third fire starter is?"

"We want Jack. He's not here, is he?" I felt the now familiar heat rise inside me, like a tidal swell that began in my belly and rose outward, upward. I embraced it, fueled it with deliberate thoughts of hatred toward Tate. I did indeed hate him, far more than I feared him.

"I'll tell you anyway." Tate's voice came from further away, in the depths of the factory. "It's me. I'm the third fire starter."

CHAPTER 14

"You!" Sylvia gasped. "How...?" She let the sentence dangle unfinished, but I knew what she was thinking. How could three diverse people have the same ability?

"Are we related?" I asked. "You, Jack and I? Is there some connection between us?"

"We're not blood relatives." His voice sounded disembodied, and it was difficult to tell from which direction it came. "However there *is* a connection."

Metal scraped and a chain rattled, a macabre sound in the darkness. Sylvia whimpered and clung tighter to me. There was some comfort in her closeness. It would have been worse to be alone.

"Mr. Tate, sir," came a slurring, heavy voice. It belonged to a man and he wasn't near us, but that's all I knew. I didn't recognize the speaker. Whispers followed as Tate and the other man exchanged words. I strained to hear, but caught nothing.

"Light something," Sylvia said, voice low.

"I can't."

"Just try it."

I flicked my fingers out. Nothing happened. I snapped and shook them, but still no heat rose, no sparks flew.

"Damn," I muttered.

Tate chuckled. "Are you trying to form a flame, Miss Smith? You ought to know by now that it's futile." He seemed to have finished his conversation with the other man, but I could see no one else in the darkness. Not even a shadow.

"Why?" Sylvia asked.

"I've tried to control it," he said. "Tried to create it when I wanted it and stop it when I didn't. I failed, time after time. As you would have too, Miss Smith."

"But—"

I pinched Sylvia's arm, and she fell silent. I didn't want her telling Tate anything that may be to our advantage. If he didn't know that Jack could start fires at will, then Jack could take him by surprise when he came. If he wasn't already there.

Oh Jack, where are you?

Someone grunted. It came from the far end of the factory. It could have come from the slurring stranger, but I didn't think so.

"Jack?" I called out at the same time Sylvia did. "Jack, is that you?"

"It's me," came Tommy's thick, sleepy voice.

"Tommy!" Sylvia let me go, but I held her back.

"Wait," I whispered.

She said nothing for a few pounding heartbeats, then called out, "Tommy? Are you all right?"

The chain rattled again, followed by more grunting. "Bloody 'ell! What's goin' on? Miss Langley? Is that you?"

"Yes," she said. "Where are you?"

"Don't know. I can't see a bloody thing. There's chains around my wrists and I can't move my legs."

Brightness flared in the depths of the factory as Tate lit a gas lamp. The small circle cast yellow light on the prone figure of Tommy lying on a bench, his wrists attached to chains and his ankles cuffed to the table. Dried blood smeared his bottom lip, and a shadowy bruise cupped one eye. Behind him stood a huge man with a jaw shaped like a brick and just as hard. His shoulders were wide and hunched as if he carried a heavy weight on them. His brow bulged over dull, vacant eyes.

"My God, what have you done to him?" Sylvia cried.

"He's a friend of yours?" Tate asked. "Ham said he was looking around the factory. I can't allow that. Who is he? Another one of Langley's so-called nephews?"

"He's our footman."

Tate tipped his head back and laughed. "Capital! So Langley's sending the servants to do his work for him?"

"Aren't you?" I said, pointing my chin at the brute behind Tommy.

"That's Ham, short for Hamley. August isn't the only one who can recruit oversized idiots to work for him."

"Who're you calling an idiot?" Tommy said, pulling on one of the chains.

"I was referring to Bollard."

Whatever Bollard was, he was not stupid. Not like Ham. Both may have perfected that vacant stare, but Bollard's couldn't always hide the shrewdness behind his eyes. I'd wager there were no thoughts of any kind in Ham's mind. If the label of idiot bothered him, he didn't show it.

"Let Tommy go," I said. "This is nothing to do with him."

"He shouldn't have been in here," Tate said.

"Why?" Sylvia asked. "It's not like there's anything worth seeing in this burnt wreck."

"Let him go!" I shouted.

Tate moved further into the fuzzy circle of light near Tommy. "Are you getting angry, Miss Smith?" He picked up the lamp and held it high in our direction. "Yes, I believe you are. Very good. I'd like to see what happens. It's been a long time since I've observed the phenomena on another."

I swallowed, and some of my anger disappeared. It wasn't the reaction I wanted. Despite his wish to study me, spitting fire from my fingertips would have come in quite handy at that moment. "Jack's not here, is he?" I said in the hope the answer would rile me again.

"No," said Tommy. "I had a good look around before this beast clobbered me." He pointed at Ham and the chain clanked against the bench.

"Jack's not here," Tate said. "I haven't seen him. What does that mean, do you suppose? Has he left? Is he lost?"

"I doubt it," Sylvia said.

I pinched her again and she flinched.

"Pity. I would have liked to see him after all this time. He was a baby when I last saw him."

He'd known Jack as a baby? Was that because Jack really was Langley's nephew and as his partner, Tate had seen him? Or was there another reason? Something to do with the fire?

Tate returned the lamp to the hook hanging from the ceiling near Tommy and stepped back into the shadows. There was only enough light to outline his silhouette. "He was a good baby on the whole, but when he threw a tantrum, he was far more frightening than any child had a right to be."

I could only imagine. "Were we born with it?" I asked.

"Hannah, now is not the time to question him about yourself," Sylvia whispered. "We must release Tommy and find Jack. Have you got a plan?"

"Yes," I lied. "I'm instigating it as we speak."

I felt her relax a little against me, which I decided was indeed part of my plan. A relaxed Sylvia could think clearer and act faster if necessary.

"Release Tommy!" I ordered Tate.

He began to move toward us through the darkness, his silhouette dimly visible until his pale, glistening face emerged from the darkness like a ghost. Sylvia gave a little squeal, and Tate growled, baring his ugly teeth. He pushed her away. It wasn't a hard shove, but she fell to the floor.

"Sylvia!" I reached for her, but Tate grabbed my arm and pulled me into his side. His breath reeked worse than rancid meat, and heat swamped me. It was like opening an oven door and being blasted by hot air. There were no sparks or flames, but it was almost too hot to bear.

"Miss Langley! Miss Smith!" Tommy tried to free himself, yanking at his chains and twisting himself about on the bench. It achieved nothing except a great deal of frustration if his grunts and curses were any indication. "What's going on, you cur?" he snarled. "If you harm them, I'll kill you!"

Tate didn't seem to hear him, or care what he'd done to Sylvia. "Hannah," he said, voice feather-soft in my ear. "Oh, Hannah. I'm so glad you've come back to me. I've been searching for you for a long time. A very long time. Sweet, little baby Hannah." He touched my hair, my cheek. I turned my face away, but he let go of my arm and grasped my jaw instead, forcing me to look at him. His fingers dug into my skin, crushing the bone. Heat and pain shot from my jaw to my neck and cheeks. I couldn't move my head, couldn't speak. "I've waited years for you. *Years.* I will not let anyone take you away this time. I need you."

The man had only one arm. Surely I could free myself. I tried pulling away, but he held my jaw too hard. My face hurt. My cheeks mashed into my teeth. I punched him in the chest and to my surprise and sheer relief, he grunted and let go.

"You little monster!" he snarled.

I raced to Sylvia's side and was about to bend down to her when a thick arm circled my waist and pulled me back. Ham. My feet rose off the ground, and the massive arm held me so tightly I felt like I was being sliced in half.

"Let go!" I screamed, clawing at Ham's arm and kicking out at Tate who stood in front of me. I missed and Ham made no sounds of pain as I shredded his shirtsleeve and drew blood.

"Hannah!" Sylvia got to her feet and ran to us. Ham deflected her with a fist to her shoulder and she fell onto the floor once more. She slid into a burnt set of drawers with a missing leg. Somehow it had managed to remain upright throughout the fire that had destroyed the factory, but a bump from Sylvia sent it crashing onto the rubble.

"Sylvia?" I called. "Are you all right?"

"Yes," came her shaking voice.

"Bloody 'ell!" Tommy growled. "Let me go! Fight like a man, you one-armed dog."

I didn't think name-calling was going to achieve much, but I didn't say. I was more worried about the brute squeezing me. I couldn't breathe.

"Easy," Tate said to Ham. "Don't kill her. I need her alive. The other two, however, are unnecessary."

Sylvia sobbed into her folded arms. Tommy's chains rattled violently and he grunted again as he tried to free himself. Ham eased his grip, but he was too big. I couldn't get away. Not by any conventional means anyway.

Get angry, get angry, get angry.

It was useless. I was much too afraid. Tears blurred my vision and dripped down my cheeks. Tommy and Sylvia were going to die because of me, and I would become a prisoner again, this time of Tate's. All because I couldn't call on my temper at will. My fear was much too powerful. I'd once thought myself brave—how wrong I'd been.

A high-pitched grunt had me opening my eyes again, just in time to see Sylvia raising a piece of ceramic pipe above her head.

But Tate had heard her too, and he turned in time to catch the pipe. He wrenched it from her grip as sparks flew from his fingers and shot in all directions. *He* had no difficulty growing angry.

Sylvia fell back onto her rear, but Tate went after her, holding the pipe like a bat. She screamed and put her hands up. I screamed. Tommy shouted and cursed, his chains rattling furiously. Still Tate descended upon her.

A small light to the right caught my attention. Flames danced atop a piece of broken wood. Tate's sparks must have set it alight. Much of the factory's contents were already burnt to ash, but there was enough left to provide fuel for another fire. Sylvia and Tommy would burn to death, if Tate didn't smash their heads in first.

He'd been distracted by the fire too, but now he turned back to Sylvia. She cowered on the floor near the fallen drawers, her face buried in her arm, her feet pulled up to make herself as small as possible. Huge, gulping sobs wracked her body.

"No," I begged Tate. "No, please don't. I'll do whatever you ask. I'll help you willingly with your research if you leave them unharmed."

"You'll help me anyway. You won't have a choice. I can't leave witnesses." He raised the pipe.

Something bright whooshed past my ear and slammed into his chest. He fell backward, crashing into burnt tables and equipment, splintering wood and sending objects flying. His eyes and mouth widened in shock. I could see his expression clearly thanks to the bright ball of fire that had sent him reeling and now set his waistcoat alight.

I turned to see the source of the fireball just as Ham let me go.

"Jack!" Sylvia cried.

Jack stood in the open doorway, sucking in deep breaths, his fists at his sides as if he would draw holstered guns. Another man stood a little behind him, his mouth ajar as he took in the scene. I was so relieved to see Jack I almost ran up and hugged him. But there was no time for that. Ham lumbered up to him and swung his massive fist. Jack easily ducked it.

"Stop!" the stranger shouted. "I am Inspector Ruxton from Scotland Yard, and I command you stop this at once!"

A policeman. Oh thank God.

But his announcement changed nothing. It was as if he weren't even there. Ham struck out at Jack, but Jack was fast and dodged it. Indeed, he was so fast it was difficult to distinguish his movements. He must have hit Ham because the man tumbled backwards, but not before he landed a punch that Jack hadn't seen coming.

Jack grunted and doubled over. The inspector rushed in

and ordered them to stop fighting, but Ham swatted him away like an annoying bee. The inspector fell to the floor near Sylvia, hitting his head on the corner of a steel box, rendering him unconscious.

She checked to see if he still breathed. "He's alive," she said. "Now what do we do?"

Tommy coughed. "Uh, ladies. Perhaps you can free me before the fire comes any closer." He coughed again and pointed his chin at the fire that had spread from those few sparks of Tate's. It was very near him. Too near.

I helped Sylvia to stand. "Get out," I ordered.

"But Tommy!"

"I'll help him." When she hesitated, I pushed her gently. "I can't burn, Sylvia, you can. Now go, and take Inspector Ruxton with you!" He was making noises on the floor and rubbing his head. If she could get him to stand, she might be able to stumble outside with him. "I can't save Tommy unless you're safe."

She glanced at Tommy and the fire, so close to him now that he'd turned his face away from the heat. His body shook with his coughs as the smoke filled the small factory. Breathing was difficult for me too, but not impossible. Not yet.

I might not be able to burn like normal people, but could I die from breathing in the smoke?

Sylvia whimpered then seemed to come to a decision she was happy with. She nodded and helped the dazed inspector to stand. Together they made it out the door, wheezing and coughing.

I headed toward Tommy, but Tate stepped in my way before I reached the bench. Sweat trickled down the edge of his hairline and dripped onto the floor. It was hot in the factory from the growing fire, but bearable, yet he looked as if he were melting.

"I won't give up this easily," he snarled, grabbing a fistful of my hair. I'd lost my hat at some point, and my wild mane had come free of its pins.

He pulled. I winced, but did not cry out. I didn't want to do or say anything that would distract Jack. He was still locked in battle with Ham and couldn't afford to lose his focus. The brute would see the opening and pound him for sure.

But why wasn't Jack using his fire on him?

"Very well," I gasped as my chest constricted with the need to breathe clean air. "I'll do as you ask. Call off your man. Let Jack and Tommy go."

Tate coughed into his shoulder. "No."

"Let them go!"

"Why would I do that?" he had to shout over the sound of wood cracking, and Jack and Ham's grunts and coughs. "It's you I want, not them."

"But Jack's like us! You need him too." The desperation in my voice betrayed me. I would try anything, say anything, to get them free. Flames crept up the legs of the bench on which Tommy lay, flirting with the bench top. He was coughing uncontrollably, trying to twist himself so that he could bury his mouth and nose in his arm to breathe. I had to get him out.

"No, Hannah," Tate said. "You're the only one I need. Only you. He's not like us. You saw."

I didn't know what he was talking about, but there was no time to think. Indeed, thinking had suddenly become very difficult as heat rolled over my skin and smoke filled my chest. Sparks spat from my fingertips and landed near the scorched hole in his waistcoat. Tate casually slapped them out with his hand.

My fury vanished as fear once more took hold. But this time I would keep my wits about me. Tommy's life depended upon it.

Tate went to grab me, and I stepped out of his reach. My bustle hit a table, halting my progress. Tate lunged.

I fumbled behind me, and my fingers touched something solid and long. I picked it up and swung it at his head. It was some kind of tool and it made a very good weapon. Tate crumpled to the floor, unconscious.

"Miss Smith!" Tommy wheezed.

I tore off a piece of my skirt at the hem and tied it around my nose and mouth, then tore off another strip. I removed the chains attached to Tommy's wrists and handed him the cloth. He tied it around the lower half of his face as I unclasped the cuffs at his ankles. The bench had caught alight and Tommy had to leap off before his clothes suffered the same fate.

He wove and ducked his way through the wrecked factory to Jack and Ham. The big fellow bled from the nose, but he didn't look any weaker. He swung at Jack, but Tommy caught his arm. He couldn't stop the momentum completely, but he did slow Ham down enough to allow Jack to punch him hard enough to daze him. Tommy and Jack were able to subdue him between them, but all three coughed violently.

My lungs screamed for fresh air. My chest hurt with the effort to breathe. Smoke made my eyes water and my mouth dry. We had to get out.

"Anyone still alive in here?" someone called from the entrance.

"Coming," I rasped as loudly as I could. Whether I was heard over the roar of the fire, I couldn't tell. Smoke and heat whirled around us. Flames flowed like a river across the ceiling, up the walls, eating everything in its path. A beam fell on the bench on which Tommy had lain, and that section of the roof caved in.

Jack ushered me to the door. He and Tommy held Ham between them, but the thug didn't struggle. I think he wanted to get out of there too. We poured out of the factory and into driving rain just as more of the roof collapsed. Four men relieved Tommy and Jack of Ham. Sylvia caught me in her arms and hugged me.

I could barely hear her soothing words above the shouts and activity of the men. There seemed to be dozens of them, some in uniform with brass helmets, others in plain workmen's clothing. They wrestled with two thick hoses spurting water onto the factory. It wasn't raining after all.

"Did you fetch them?" I managed to rasp out between my coughs.

She nodded and looked over my shoulder. "Tommy, where's Jack?"

I spun round. Tommy was there, bent over and sucking in air. Jack was nowhere to be seen.

"He's gone inside!" I cried. I tried to pull away, but Sylvia held me back and Tommy blocked the way. "I have to go in! He's gone for Tate. Let me go, Sylvia, I can help him!"

"He can do it alone," she said. "Or not at all. I wouldn't care if that villain died in there. Hopefully the smoke will kill him if the fire will not."

I wasn't sure I cared either, but that wasn't the point. Would Jack abandon the task if it proved hopeless? Or would he try until he could try no more?

"I won't burn," I said, my voice high, desperate. "Let me help him."

"No," Tommy said. "You may not burn, but the smoke'll get you." He coughed to emphasize the point.

"But it'll get Jack too," I said on a whimper. "He can't die in there. He can't!" It wasn't until I tasted salt on my lip that I realized I was crying.

Sylvia held me tightly and Tommy hovered nearby, ordering the firemen to spray directly through the door. Moments ticked by. I was soaked. We all were, our clothes plastered to our bodies, our hair bedraggled. I didn't care. I just wanted to see him again. He had to be all right. Had to be.

I needed him.

Finally he staggered out carrying an unconscious Tate across his shoulders as if he were a log. Two firemen took him and Jack stumbled forward, coughing over and over. Tommy helped him to the side of the house, out of the way, and set him on the ground. Sylvia and I knelt beside him. His lower lip had begun to swell and blood dripped from a cut above his eye. His face was blackened from the soot, as was Tommy's. Mine must have been too, but I didn't care about my appearance. I gently pushed Jack's hair off his forehead, and my fingers immediately began to glow.

He caught my hand anyway and pressed the palm to his lips. He suppressed a cough and gently kissed the skin at my wrist. Heat rushed through my limbs and I pulled away just in time. A large spark shot from my fingertips and sizzled in the damp earth. I sat back on my haunches, breathing heavily.

Jack smiled ruefully. "I couldn't help myself. I'm so relieved you're all right."

"I'm rather glad you're alive too," I said and grinned. If I threw my arms around him, would we combust? I wanted to, so much, that I was almost prepared to try it.

"What about us?" Tommy said. "Aren't you glad your cousin and I are alive?"

"Would you like a kiss too?" Jack asked him.

Tommy sniffed. "Don't think that'll get you off. I'm bloody angry at you for going back in there for that monster."

Monster. Tate was indeed one, in every sense. It was also the word he'd used to describe me.

I sat near Jack and pulled my knees up to my chest. It was a very unladylike pose, but I didn't care. "I'm sorry," I said. "I'm so sorry. I couldn't... I was too scared..."

"Don't," Jack said. "It's not your fault."

"But I should have been able to do something. Something like what you did with that fireball."

"You haven't learned to access the fire at will yet."

Would I ever?

"Jack's right," Sylvia said, circling her arm around me. "You did everything you could. You freed Tommy on your own." She hugged me and I hugged her back.

"You did save me in there," Tommy said quietly. I looked up to see his warm eyes blinking at me. They were filled with tears that didn't spill. "Thank you, Miss Smith."

"Perhaps you can call me Hannah now," I said.

"Right then, Miss Hannah." He suddenly grinned. "May I make a request?"

"Of course."

"Can you please not leave the rescue 'til the last moment next time?"

"I don't plan on there being a next time."

"With you and Jack around?" Sylvia said. "I think you're being overly optimistic."

The man I'd seen enter the factory behind Jack, Inspector Ruxton, came up to us. He too was wet and he wore no hat, having lost it in the factory. A few strands of brown hair clung to his otherwise bald head. "That was quite a scene in there. How'd you get that flame ball so quick then, eh, Mr. Langley? It seemed to come from nowhere. You some sort of magician?"

"It's a device," Jack said. "I keep it in my pocket for emergencies."

"Really? Can I see it?"

"I lost it in the fire."

"Shame. I've got an interest in new inventions." He seemed to believe Jack's explanation, thank goodness. "So, that one-armed man...is he the fellow you told me about? The one you accuse of stealing your uncle's papers?"

"Yes," Jack said, standing. "His name is Reuben Tate."

"I, uh, I'm sorry I didn't believe you when you first came to the station, sir. It's just that I, uh, thought it better to leave it to your local constabulary."

"I'm glad I was able to convince you in the end."

"Not sure I'm so glad." The inspector gingerly touched the back of his head.

"Did you search the house?"

"My men are doing it now. So far, no luck. You'd better give me the name of your witness after all. There's no avoiding it now, I'm afraid."

Jack nodded. "His name is Patrick O'Dwyer."

Sylvia shifted her weight. Tommy cleared his throat.

"Patrick's dead," he said gently. "We found out yesterday. That's why we came here, to warn you."

Jack sat back down beside me and drew up his knees. He dragged his hands through his hair and lowered his head.

"I'm sorry." I wanted to stroke his hair and draw him into my arms, but it would only end in sparks and I didn't want the inspector to see, or to start something I couldn't stop.

Jack thumped a fist into the ground. "He told me Tate was dangerous. I should have listened."

"We weren't to know how dangerous," I said. "No one could have guessed he was a murderer."

"And arsonist," the inspector said, nodding at the factory. The blaze was under control, but the brigade-men continued to pour water on it. "The Senior Fireman told me this place has been set alight numerous times and recently too."

That would explain the new furniture and painted walls in the house. "How many?" I asked.

"Eight that I know of," said a man as he passed us. He was dressed in one of the brass helmets and woolen tunics of the firemen.

"Come inside and tell me everything," Inspector Ruxton said to us.

We walked single-file back along the path at the side of the house to the front door, leaving enough space for the firemen and their hoses to pass us. It was early afternoon, but the heavy clouds obscured the sun and allowed little light through. Two horse-drawn fire engines were positioned near the street-plug connected to the city's water supply. Steam hissed and spat from the brass cylinders, pumping the water to the hoses. Several workmen from the nearby factories helped, and others stood by and watched Tate being led to a waiting coach by a constable. Ham was bundled into another by four policemen. Despite having his hands tied, he managed to knock over one of the constables with a bump of his massive shoulder. It took some effort and a lot of foul language, but the others eventually got him into the cabin.

Tate was more sedate. He simply stared at me with such

longing in his gaze that I shivered, despite the heat still coursing through me. He must have seen because his top lip curled up in a distorted smile.

Jack positioned himself between Tate and me. "Take him away," he growled.

We went inside and gave our version of events to the inspector, leaving out only the details of how Tate started the fire. Of course none of us had seen how he did it, and the inspector didn't dwell on that aspect. He was more interested in the fact that Tate had chained Tommy up and wanted to kidnap me.

"A madman," he muttered as he dipped his pen in an inkwell held by one of his constables. He wrote something down in his notebook then blew on it to dry the ink. "Are you four returning to Frakingham tonight?" he asked.

"Tomorrow," Jack said. "We'll stay at Claridges tonight. The ladies will be tired."

"The ladies would like to go shopping," Sylvia corrected.

When all the men looked at her, she merely shrugged. "You cannot expect us to spend another moment in these garments. I'm sure we can organize new dresses from our rooms. It's what all the refined ladies do."

"For once, I agree with you," Jack said. "We all require new clothes. If you need us, Inspector, you can find us at Claridges."

We headed outside and skirted the fire engines to reach Olsen and the carriage. We set off, and Tommy alighted at the stables where he'd left the brougham. We three drove on to the heart of London. Jack had offered to get a room for Tommy at the salubrious hotel too, but he'd refused saying he'd feel too awkward in a "toff place." He and Olsen were to stay at an inn they knew nearby.

***

I slept solidly that night and into the next day. All three of us did. The rest of the day and part of the next was busy with fittings and fabrics. Dressmakers and milliners came to us, and by the third day, they had clothes and hats ready for our journey home.

Home. Yes, I supposed it was, in a way. There was nothing for me at Windamere anymore, but I now knew I at least had friends in Jack, Sylvia and Tommy. Frakingham was the only place I belonged.

I was grateful to be finally leaving Claridges. Not that the hotel wasn't exquisite, our every need and comfort met, but because I wanted to be alone with Jack again at Frakingham. We'd been surrounded by others ever since the fire, and I had so many things I wanted to talk to him about before we saw his uncle again.

He rode with Sylvia and me inside the cabin on the journey back. Olsen drove because Tommy had left the morning after the fire to report back to Langley. At first I was glad I wasn't going to be near him when he found out what Tate had almost done to us, but then I changed my mind. Seeing Langley's first reaction may have said a great deal about his character as well as his intentions.

"Well," said Sylvia on a breath. "I'm glad that's over."

London grew smaller in the distance, the miasma that hung over the city merely a brown stain on the horizon. I didn't dislike the place, but I didn't want to return there in a hurry. Frakingham at least had fresh air and open spaces, although its moodiness was something I wasn't yet used to.

"There'll be a trial," Jack said. "We'll all be called as witnesses. It's not quite over yet."

"I can endure a trial to see that man swing," Sylvia said. "He and his creature."

"They don't actually hang people in public anymore, Syl."

"You know what I mean. They deserve to be hanged. You shouldn't have gotten Tate out, Jack."

He lowered his gaze and said nothing.

"And now that I think about it," she went on, "why didn't you throw one of those fireballs at the thug, Ham? You could have saved yourself all those bruises."

Jack fingered his swollen lip. The cut above his eye had closed, but it still looked raw and would be for some time.

His knuckles too were grazed and must be sore.

"That's a good question," I said to Jack. "You threw one at Tate, but not Ham. Why?"

"It would set his clothes alight and burn him," he said.

"So?" Sylvia said. "The man was horrible. He doesn't deserve our sympathies or your consideration."

"You think that now," he said. "But if *you* were the one inflicting the fireball and you had to watch a man burn alive, would you think the same then?"

"Yes."

He shook his head and turned to the window. From the distant gaze reflected in the glass, I guessed that he wasn't actually seeing any of the scenery that slipped past. "It's the screaming that gets to you first," he said. "Even a man as large and strong as Ham has a high-pitched scream when his skin is exposed to intense heat. After the screams comes the smell. Burning flesh has a distinctive odor, Syl. It's not very pleasant. You wouldn't like it."

She fell silent and pulled the collar of her new fur coat closed at the throat.

"I saw someone burn to death once," he went on. "I wouldn't wish it on my worst enemy."

"You, Hannah and Tate can't burn though, can you?" Sylvia asked.

Jack shook his head. "I know I can't. Hannah? Did you feel anything in there? Did your skin hurt?"

I shook my head. "I felt nothing on the outside, only the inside when Tate touched me." The memory of him stroking my face made me want to scrub myself clean again. There had been no desire in the touch, not the sort between a man and a woman, but it had been filled with a kind of longing that I'd never seen before and had not known could exist. "He was boiling. To me he felt hotter than the fire."

Jack leaned forward and lifted a hand. He stroked a strand of my hair that had fallen out of the pins and dangled near my face. Although I instantly warmed, there were no sparks. It seemed it was only actual contact between us that produced those.

I smiled and he smiled back. "Thank you for rescuing me," I said.

"My pleasure." He continued to stroke my hair. I liked it, liked him near me, but it took every ounce of self-control not to lean into that hand and feel it cupping my cheek, caressing my lips.

Sylvia, not looking at us, shuddered. "Thank goodness Tate's gone. Finally we can resume some normalcy at Freak House."

"Normalcy," Jack said with a lopsided smile. "Is that what you're calling it now?"

CHAPTER 15

Langley met us in the courtyard on our arrival. He sat in his wheelchair, his hands folded in his lap. Bollard stood behind him, staring straight ahead. When we strolled up to them, Langley's hands moved from his lap to the wheels as if he would push himself forward, but quickly returned to his lap again. He scrutinized each of us in turn before finally settling on Jack's swollen lip.

"You're back," was all he said. "Tommy told me you were successful in your endeavors."

"Oh Uncle, it was awful!" Sylvia bent down and hugged him. It was awkward with him sitting, and she seemed not to know where to put her arms. Langley was equally ill at ease. He patted her back as if she were a puppy that had just fetched his slippers for the first time.

She wiped the tears from her cheeks then went to move away. He caught her hand and kept her at his side.

"It's cold out here," he said. "Mrs. Moore will bring tea to us in the parlor. Tell me everything there."

He continued to hold Sylvia's hand as Bollard wheeled him inside. He must have been concerned after all and relieved to see us again. The only time I'd seen him outside, or indeed downstairs, was on the night of the fire. Neither his old room nor his new one were on the ground floor. He must have seen us coming up the drive and had Bollard bring both him and the wheelchair down to meet us. My eyes pricked with tears, until I realized that he hadn't been eager to see *us* again, only his niece and nephew. Or perhaps only Sylvia. Aside from frowning at Jack's cuts and bruises, he'd not paid his nephew much attention.

We sat in the small parlor that we'd been using since the night of the fire. It no longer smelled musty. A low fire warmed it, keeping the chill out of the air I suppose, although I'd never known what a chill really felt like. Some of Sylvia's paintings now decorated the walls and her embroidered cushions sat plump and inviting on the sofa. Tea arrived shortly after us, brought in by Tommy, not Mrs. Moore. It was odd to see him all stiff and formal again. Aside from a quick glance at each of us, he resumed his blank, footman's gaze. I found it most irritating.

"It's good to see you, Tommy," I said, smiling. "Have you suffered any ill effects from the fire?"

"No, Miss Smith."

"I thought we agreed you would call me Hannah now."

He splashed tea over the side of a cup and looked at Langley. "I, uh, don't feel right calling you anything other than what's proper."

"I agree," Sylvia said. She lifted her chin, but it didn't hide the quick glance she shot at Tommy and the slight blush to her cheeks. "Whatever transpired in London should remain there."

"How can you say that?" I said. "The four of us formed a bond at Tate's factory. You can't deny it."

"She'll try her hardest," Jack muttered.

"Circumstances in London were...unique," she said. "Never to be repeated. Besides, just because we all endured a nasty experience together doesn't mean we can allow social mores to lapse. I know you don't fully understand the importance of keeping everyone in their place, Hannah, having lived your entire life in an attic among a total of two people. You'll simply have to trust me. It's important. Isn't that right, Uncle?" She faced her uncle, but her gaze slid between him and Tommy.

The footman was too busy pouring the tea to notice, but he did seem more rigid than usual.

"Social order is everything," Langley agreed. "The opposite is chaos."

Behind him, Bollard's nostrils flared. Tommy left, carrying the tray with him.

"Tell me what happened," Langley said. "Tommy informs me they arrived before you, Jack. Where were you?"

"I'd gone to the Harborough constabulary immediately after leaving here," Jack said. "I had to wait for that fool of an inspector to return, and then I wasted more time trying to convince him to come with me to London. He refused." He shook his head. "I wish I hadn't bothered."

"You tried to do the right thing," I said. Sylvia and I had already told him so in the carriage when he spoke of his reasons for his delay, but he hadn't accepted it then and it still seemed to rankle now.

"I went to the Hackney Wick authorities as soon as I arrived in London," he went on. "There was no point confronting Tate without a witness. I had to wait at the police station there too, and then when the inspector did return, I spent some time apprising him of the case against Tate. He agreed to come with me, albeit reluctantly."

"It was a good thing he did," I said.

"When we arrived, we heard noises coming from the factory. The fire had already taken hold, and Tate..." He swallowed heavily and looked at me.

"Tell me about the fire," Langley asked.

"Tate started that," I said. "He accidentally emitted sparks from his fingers. You didn't tell us he was a fire starter too. It would have helped, you know."

"Perhaps," Langley said and sipped his tea. I was reminded of Tate casually drinking tea in his parlor and avoiding our questions. The similarity sent a shiver down my spine.

"That's why he wanted Hannah, isn't it?" Jack asked. "Because he's a fire starter too and he wanted to...study her." From the lack of shock on his face, I suspected he'd been thinking about it the entire journey home. As had I.

Sylvia, however, gasped and almost dropped her teacup. "You think he wanted to dissect her to find a cure?" She turned quite pale. "Now I regret reading that book on biology last year."

"I'm not sure about dissection," Langley said. "But I do think he wanted to use her in some way." He frowned into his teacup. Something troubled him and from the look on his face, I'd wager he'd just thought of something he *didn't* know the answer to. The scientist in him must hate it.

Jack rose and stood over his uncle, his clenched fists at his sides. When he spoke, it was low and his jaw hardly moved. "You knew Tate wanted to use Hannah and yet you let her come after me?"

"I didn't *let* Hannah go," Langley said. "She went without permission. In case you haven't noticed, the girl has a will of her own and tends to follow it without thinking things through."

"I resent the accusation," I said. "I would not have gone if I'd known Tate was a fire starter himself." Probably not. Maybe. "Perhaps you ought to keep us all apprised of the villains you've fallen out with, Mr. Langley. Keeping secrets helps no one."

"Are you quite finished?" he said.

I sipped my tea. Jack moved to the window and leaned against the sill. He stared out to the abbey ruins beyond. Perhaps he was desperate to get into the cool air, to exercise the stiffness from his joints and the demons from his mind.

"How did Tate know about me?" I asked Langley. "When I introduced myself, he seemed to recognize my name, as I think you did when I first told you I was Hannah Smith. But if Tate connected me to being a fire starter, shouldn't he have thought my name was Violet, as you presumed?"

"Hannah Smith was the name of...someone we used to know. I didn't know you'd been given that name too. You were a baby when Reuben Tate and I first met you. You had no name then."

What parents didn't give their child a name? My parents, it seemed. Parents who died soon after the birth of their child.

"Is Hannah Smith my mother?"

"No."

"Then who is she?"

He didn't answer and I let the matter drop. There were more pressing questions to ask. "Is that why you want me? To study me and find a cure for Jack?"

"You are different than Jack. There'd be no point." It wasn't quite a no. "Tell me, was Reuben interested in Jack? Did he...want him the way he wanted you?"

I shook my head. "Just me."

Jack looked from me to Langley. He crossed his arms. "Why is that significant?"

"Your abilities are different than Reuben's and Hannah's," Langley said. "You can control your fire. They cannot."

"You've led us to believe that Hannah will learn."

"That's because I think she will, in time."

"But I didn't need to learn," Jack said quietly. "It's always been instinctive. I never questioned it too much, never thought too deeply about how it happened. Until I met you," he said to me. "Now I question everything."

"Why are we different?" I asked Langley. "Why did Tate want me and not Jack?"

"I can only guess it's because he thinks the cure for it is within you, not Jack. As to why Jack is different..." He sipped his tea. "I cannot say."

"He said he knew Jack as a baby. That means you did too. Is that because Jack really is your nephew or because he was part of an experiment?"

"I don't owe you an explanation about Jack, Hannah."

I expected Jack to question him further, but he did not. Why?

"Why does Tate want to be cured?" Sylvia asked, speaking after a long silence.

"I suppose because of the unpredictability of it. It can make going about one's daily business difficult."

"That is rather an understatement," I muttered. "Do you know why we three have this ability in the first place? There must be a reason."

Langley shrugged one shoulder. "I cannot say."

"Did you perform tests on us as children?"

"No."

"Was it something to do with a drug you were developing? Did you...change us somehow?"

"I did nothing of the sort. You've read too many of those horror novels Sylvia likes so much. I am not Dr. Frankenstein."

No, but sometimes I had the feeling I was the monster of the story.

"Did it have something to do with the Society For Supernatural Activity?" Jack asked, moving back toward our cluster of chairs.

Langley inclined his head. "He told you about it?"

"Who are they?"

"A group of men and women interested in the paranormal, those things which can't be explained by scientific means. Yet."

"You don't believe in the supernatural?" I asked.

He lifted his gaze to mine and held it. "I do believe, Hannah. I also think science can help us understand strange phenomena. It was an area I wanted to explore when I belonged to the Society years ago. Tate also belonged, and we researched some matters together. That's how we met."

"What matters?"

"The existence of spirits, angels, demons, that sort of thing."

"Demons!" Sylvia cried. Her hand fluttered to her chest.

"Good lord. Ghosts I can accept, but demons? Surely not."

Langley didn't look at her. He didn't look at any of us. Bollard's hand curled around one handle of the wheelchair. The knuckles went white for a moment then he pulled away.

"Do they exist?" I asked. My heart raced. I didn't know when it had begun to beat so furiously, but it seemed to want to know the answer to the question very badly.

"I've found no proof to indicate they don't."

"Isn't that the wrong way around? Shouldn't you be proving that they do?"

"Members of the Society begin with the viewpoint that the supernatural is real."

"Do you still belong to the Society?" Jack asked.

"No. However, I have kept in touch with some current members. They come to me with questions every now and again."

"Why you?"

"I *am* the foremost microbiologist in the country."

And the one with the highest opinion of himself.

"Enough questions," he said, setting his teacup down on the table beside him. "Bollard."

"Wait." I leapt off the sofa and rested my hand on his wheelchair arm. If Bollard wanted to push forward, he could, but he did not. "How did you know I was at Windamere Manor when Tate didn't?"

He shook his head. "Bollard. Forward."

Jack put his hand on the other wheelchair arm. Bollard didn't try to move off. It seemed I wasn't the only one who wanted to know the answer, but to have Bollard on my side in this was a complete surprise.

Langley drew in a deep breath and let it out slowly. "I sent you there to keep you away from Tate when you were a baby. I knew I couldn't trust him with you, knew he wanted to use you. I gave you to Lord Wade. He was a member of our Society and one of the few I could trust with a child's welfare."

"His way of caring for a child included locking her in the

attic for years," Jack said. "Perhaps you should have tried harder to find someone else."

"I didn't expect him to do that, nor did I find out until very recently."

"Why did Lord Wade keep me *and* his daughter locked up in the attic?" I asked. "Me, I understand. I was dangerous and I wasn't his child. But Violet? It doesn't make sense."

"You'd have to ask him that. She's nothing to do with me."

"Very well." One day I would do exactly that. "Did you hypnotize me and give me narcolepsy?"

"No."

I sighed. Another thing to ask Wade. "So why kidnap me now, Mr. Langley? Does it have anything to do with Tate suddenly needing me?"

"He's always needed you. There's nothing sudden about it."

I was a little shocked and withdrew my hand from the chair arm.

"But not quite as badly as he needs her now," Jack muttered. "Because he's known where you live for some time, August, yet he only stole your papers a few nights ago. He was looking for her, wasn't he? Looking for some way to find her? Isn't that right?"

"I don't know. You'd have to ask Tate that question."

I didn't plan on going anywhere near Tate. He would have to hang before I would completely relax again. "He thought I was dead," I said, recalling his words. "So I don't think he stole your papers in the hope of finding me. I think he was looking for a way to cure himself. He hoped you'd kept working on it. Indeed, he assumed you had."

Langley looked surprised that I knew that much. "Perhaps."

"So why did you send Jack to kidnap me *now*?" I asked.

"The governess contacted me and asked me to remove you."

"Miss Levine?" I'd known she was party to the secret that

had been kept from me, but I'd not known she was aware of the connection to Langley.

"She claimed that living in the attic was no life for either you or your friend."

"That seems rather too kind of her," I muttered. And yet she didn't hate me, nor I her. We'd clashed often, but hate was a strong word that didn't fit our relationship.

"I wish she'd told me you were the companion and not the daughter," he said, shaking his head. "When Bollard told me that he'd heard there were two of you confined to the attic, I naturally assumed *you* were being passed off as his daughter, and *she* the companion."

"*Is* Vi his daughter?"

"I don't know."

"She may be illegitimate," Sylvia said. "Perhaps he's ashamed of her and what he did. What do you know of Lady Wade, Hannah? Did she look like Lady Violet?"

"I don't know anything about her." Indeed I was beginning to question everything I thought I did know.

"It was fortunate that you got the right girl in the end, Jack," Sylvia said cheerfully. "I'm certainly glad we have Hannah and not the other one. She sounds like she can't be trusted if she was indeed part of Hannah's kidnapping." The fact that most of the people in the room had been part of my kidnapping seemed to have escaped her notice.

"That's not what you first thought when you found out we didn't have an earl's daughter under our roof," Jack said.

She sniffed. "Don't be ridiculous." She smiled at me and patted my arm. "Hannah is delightful company. I can't imagine anyone else I'd rather have as my friend."

I smiled at her, but it wavered a little when I recalled Vi saying something very similar.

"Why *did* you take her and not Violet?" Sylvia asked Jack.

"The governess described the one to collect, but gave me no name. She simply called her 'that fire girl.' Nor did she tell me the one I wanted was the companion and not the lady." The color of his eyes deepened as his gaze held mine.

"Besides, I felt a connection with Hannah. It was like I was being pulled toward her. What better evidence is there that we are alike?"

"Then you must have felt the same connection to Tate."

Jack said nothing. Langley, Sylvia and I turned to him. Even Bollard's gaze slid to Jack's.

"No," Jack finally said. "I felt nothing around Tate. Only you, Hannah."

A little jolt shot through me and my face heated. *Only you.* I smiled at him, and his lips quirked up at the edges. Then he frowned and looked down at his hands.

"Those children have to be gone by tomorrow," Langley said.

"What children?" Sylvia asked. "Oh, yes, Patrick's friends. Your friends," she said to Jack.

We'd told him about the children coming to us, and how they had no adult to care for them. He'd expressed his concern that they might wind up thieving to survive. We'd come to the conclusion on the journey home that something needed to be done, but we'd not decided what.

"Can't they stay here?" I asked.

"Not all of them!" Sylvia said. "There's far too many, especially with half the house in ruins."

"They're noisy and disruptive," Langley said. "I can't work with the two of them running about, let alone dozens."

"We'll need to find somewhere for them in London," Jack said.

"We ain't going to the workhouse!" The boy, Sniffles, stood in the doorway. He wiped the back of his hand across his nose. He looked neater than the first day he'd arrived. His hair had been combed flat and he wore clean clothes that were too large but looked warm.

"I won't let you end up at the workhouse, Davey," Jack said, going to him. "There must be a charity school you can attend."

Davey pulled a face. "I hate school."

Jack made as if to clip him over the ear, but nudged him

affectionately instead. "Go on. Go find Tommy and annoy him. Let us sort out where you'll go."

"You sort it out, Jack," the boy said. He wrinkled his nose at Langley and Bollard. "Not them." He darted off.

Frowning, Jack watched him go.

"How many more of them are there?" I asked.

"Dozens. I'd been sending Patrick money, and he was supposed to be taking care of them." He came back inside and shut the door. "There's no room for all of them here, even if they weren't disruptive, but there's no one to look after them in London. They'll have to be separated and families found for each of them."

"Is it necessary to separate them?" I knew what it was like to be wrenched from the only family I knew, and I was eighteen. It would be horrible to do that to little children.

"Is that even possible?" Sylvia asked.

"It is with the right amount of money," Jack said. "No one will take in extra children without an incentive."

"I'm not sure you'd encourage people with good hearts that way," I said. "The greedy ones, on the other hand, would be falling over themselves."

Langley grunted. "I'll provide whatever is needed."

Bollard said something to Langley with his hands. The rapid movements were smooth and elegant, his fingers dexterous in their twisting and pointing. I'd never seen him communicate with Langley, it had always been the other way around. It made the servant more human, but only just.

When Bollard finished, Langley closed his eyes. He didn't open them or speak for some time, and I grew anxious that he would dismiss us all and make the boys leave Frakingham. What Jack would do in that situation was anyone's guess.

"There's a charity school in London," Langley finally said, opening his eyes. "Its patroness is a lady named Emily Beaufort, the wife of Jacob Beaufort. She's a most interesting woman, quite the sensation about eight years or so ago."

"Why?"

"She was a girl of dubious parentage who married the son

of a prominent viscount."

"Is that all?" Sylvia scoffed. "It may be unusual, perhaps a curiosity even, but to describe it as a sensation...hardly."

"She can also communicate with ghosts."

Sylvia snorted through her nose. "Are you serious?"

"Have you ever known me to joke?"

She paled. "No. But are you certain she's not a charlatan? I've read of many accounts in the papers where spirit mediums have turned out to be false."

"You mean like the one you visited last year?" Jack asked.

Sylvia gave him a withering glare. "I would have thought a viscount's daughter-in-law would conduct herself in a manner befitting her station."

"So would I," Langley said.

"What has her ability to see ghosts got to do with the charity school?" I asked.

"Nothing," Langley said. "The two facts aren't connected. Why don't you write to her, Sylvia, and request she look into the situation with the children?"

She brightened, and I suspected she was glad to be given something to do. She bustled out, and I followed. Jack remained behind.

I went to my room to freshen up after the journey and ate a sandwich of cold meat delivered by one of the maids. I tried to rest too, but couldn't. The events of London were too fresh, too frightening. I went in search of Jack instead and wasn't surprised to find him near the lake. He stood with his back to me. The breeze ruffled the ends of his hair, but otherwise, he was very still. Serene. I didn't want to disturb him, so I turned to go.

"Wait, Hannah." He was beside me in the moment it took me to turn back. "I'm glad you came. I wanted to talk to you."

The now familiar warmth of desire spread through my body, lighting every part of me along the way. It didn't feel wrong or uncomfortable, but so very delicious.

"Oh?" I whispered. "What about?"

"About my past." He looked toward the ruins. "Come with me."

We sat side by side on a low, crumbling wall of the old abbey. Jack's feet touched the ground, mine did not. I waited for him to begin again, even though I knew what he wanted to say. Tommy had already told me some of it, but I wanted to hear it from Jack's lips. He had to do this on his own, without prompting. It must be wholly his own decision.

It meant so much more that way.

"I used to live with those children in London. Tommy and I both did. I was one of them. An orphan with no home, nowhere to go. I don't remember a time before that. I had no family, or so I thought. Tate confirmed that they knew me as a baby, so that's something at least. Perhaps I really am Langley's nephew, although he won't say how I came to live on the streets."

"You've asked?"

"Yes. When I first got here, I would ask every day for information about my parents, my background, but he would give only evasive answers until finally he snapped altogether and threatened to send me back to the streets. I couldn't go back to that life. Not then. And now I'm just used to not knowing. I've decided I don't *want* to know."

Because he might not like the answer. I nodded, understanding completely. "Tell me about being on the streets with the other children."

"When we were small, the bigger children took care of us. We thieved for them, picked pockets, whatever we could to survive as a group. They were like a family to me, I suppose, but life was hard and some of those older children...they were cruel. But not to me. I had these." He waggled his fingers. "As I grew older and I realized the power it gave me, I began to take charge. Since I was the only one who could keep the entire group warm in winter, no one argued against me. Besides, I was a capable fighter by then."

I nodded. I saw how good he was against Ham. That man had been huge, but Jack had held him off and got some swift punches in.

"We had to steal to live," he said. "It never bothered me much. It was just something we did to survive. Then one day Bollard showed up and everything changed." He huffed out a wry laugh. "Most of the children were terrified of him. He gave me a note. It told me to go with Bollard, and I'd be given all the food I wanted and a warm bed. The warm bed wasn't so enticing, but the food was. Tommy insisted on coming with me, and when August tried to send him away, I refused to stay. If he had to go, I would too. August gave in, grudgingly."

"What explanation did Langley give for thinking you were his nephew?"

"He gave none. He said I was his nephew and my name was no longer Cutler. When I asked him how he found me, he said he simply asked the right people. Like I said, evasive answers."

Neither of us spoke for a long time, but something bothered me. I didn't know how Jack would react when I asked, but I suspected it was something he'd already considered so I asked anyway. "Do you think Mr. Langley made a mistake and got the wrong boy?"

He shook his head. "He questioned me thoroughly about my parents. Their names, where they were from, what they looked like. I didn't remember them, but I own a knife with a distinctive handle. I assume it came from them as it's always been in my possession. I showed August, and he said he recognized it."

"May I see it?"

He blinked at me from beneath the hair that had tumbled over his forehead. "It's in my room."

We hopped off the wall and walked as close to each other as possible without actually touching. It was enough to warm but not overheat me. Neither of us wore coats or gloves, and I doubted I ever would again. Miss Levine had tried to force me, but I no longer saw the point.

"Jack," I said.

"Hmmm?"

"I'm so glad you abducted me."

He chuckled. "So am I."

"And thank you for telling me about your childhood."

"It was either I tell you or you'd find out from Sylvia anyway. She has a loose tongue."

I laughed and hoped he never found out it was Tommy who'd given me more information than Sylvia.

I gazed up at Frakingham House ahead. The builders had begun to erect scaffolding on the eastern wing in preparation for the repairs, and already the network of wood and steel looked like a complex spider's web. A man stood on the driveway, his head tilted up to look at the burnt section of the house. A suitcase sat at his feet.

"Who is that?" I asked.

Jack squinted. "Gladstone?"

"Good lord, it is. Samuel!" I called.

He turned and I waved. He left his suitcase and came to meet us. "Good afternoon, Lady Violet, Mr. Langley." He tipped his hat. "What a pleasure it is to see you again."

"Actually, my name is Hannah." At his raised brows, I added, "It's a long story to be told over tea. So what brings you to Frakingham?"

"I hear they call this place Freak House." He shot a grim glance at the building. "I thought it might be somewhere I would fit in."

Jack crossed his arms. "You mean to stay?"

"I hoped to speak to Mr. August Langley and propose a research project."

"How exciting," I said. "Are you not working with Dr. Werner anymore?"

Samuel frowned. "No."

"What makes you think August would be interested in your proposal, Mr. Gladstone?" Jack asked.

"Call me Samuel. I believe your uncle has an interest in neuroscience. I thought perhaps he may want the chance to work with a real hypnotist."

"August is very busy," Jack said. "And neuroscience is not his field of expertise."

"I'd like to speak to him anyway."

Jack held out his hand for Samuel to go ahead. We entered the house and Tommy showed Samuel up to Langley's room. Jack, Sylvia and I waited in the parlor.

"How odd," Sylvia said. "I wonder why he left Dr. Werner's employ."

"Perhaps he was thrown out," Jack said.

Sylvia eyed him suspiciously. "You don't appear to like Mr. Gladstone very much. Why?"

Jack looked to me then away. "He's too self-assured."

It sounded so absurd coming from someone of equal confidence that I snorted a laugh. He glared at me.

Finally Samuel returned. His smile was so broad it almost stretched to both ears.

"What did he say?" Sylvia asked.

"He said I may stay here while I conduct my research."

Sylvia clapped her hands. "Splendid. It appears our little household is growing."

"This is good news," I said, lifting my eyebrow at Jack in a challenge.

After a moment, he sighed and clapped Samuel on the shoulder. "Welcome to Freak House."

LOOK OUT FOR

Playing With Fire

The second book in the first FREAK HOUSE TRILOGY.

Hannah and Jack learn about their pasts and fall in love, but Tate's escape from prison puts their lives at risk.

To be notified when C.J. has a new release, sign up to her newsletter. Send an email to cjarcher.writes@gmail.com

Interact with the characters from Freak House on Tumblr.
http://freakhouseresidents.tumblr.com

ABOUT THE AUTHOR

C.J. Archer has loved history and books for as long as she can remember. She worked as a librarian and technical writer until she was able to channel her twin loves by writing historical fiction. She has won and placed in numerous romance writing contests, including taking home RWAustralia's Emerald Award in 2008 for the manuscript that would become her novel *Honor Bound*. Under the name Carolyn Scott, she has published contemporary romantic mysteries, including *Finders Keepers Losers Die*, and *The Diamond Affair*. After spending her childhood surrounded by the dramatic beauty of outback Queensland, she lives today in suburban Melbourne, Australia, with her husband and their two children.

She loves to hear from readers. You can contact her in one of these ways:
Website: www.cjarcher.com
Email: cjarcher.writes@gmail.com
Facebook: www.facebook.com/CJArcherAuthorPage

Printed in Great Britain
by Amazon.co.uk, Ltd.,
Marston Gate.